THE PERFECT GOLDEN CIRCLE

Fiction

Male Tears

The Offing

These Darkening Days

The Gallows Pole

Turning Blue

Beastings

Pig Iron

Richard

Non-Fiction

Under the Rock

THE PERFECT GOLDEN CIRCLE

A NOVEL

BENJAMIN MYERS

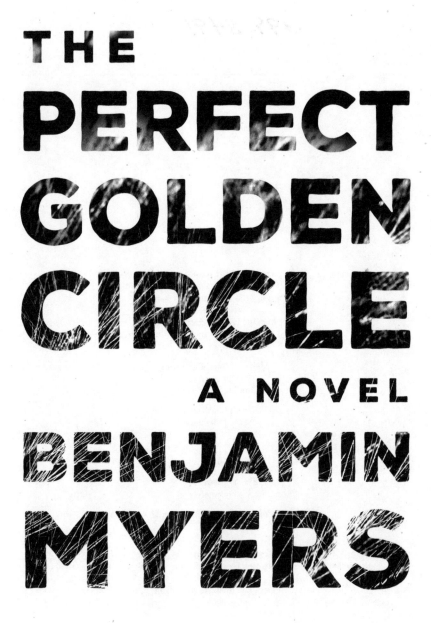 MELVILLE HOUSE
BROOKLYN • LONDON

399 8491

THE PERFECT GOLDEN CIRCLE

Copyright © Benjamin Myers, 2022
All rights reserved
First Melville House Printing: May 2022
First Published in Great Britain by Bloomsbury Circus, 2022

Melville House Publishing
46 John Street
Brooklyn, NY 11201

mhpbooks.com
@melvillehouse

ISBN: 978-1-61219-958-0

ISBN: 978-1-61219-959-7
(eBook)

Library of Congress Control Number: 2022931506

Extract from 'Groping' in *Collected Poems, 1945–1990* by R.S. Thomas, reprinted with kind permission by Orion Publishing Group Ltd, Copyright © R.S. Thomas, 2000

Designed by Beste M. Doğan

Printed in the United States of America

2 4 6 8 10 9 7 5 3 1

A catalog record for this book is available from the Library of Congress

For fellow travellers
Michele and Elliot Rashman

Sometimes a strange light
shines, purer than the moon,
casting no shadow, that is
the halo upon the bones
of the pioneers who died for truth.

—R. S. Thomas

CONTENTS

SOUTHERN ENGLAND
1989

There are still fields in England so vast that you can walk alongside them or across them – or through them – for an hour or more and feel like you have not moved an inch.

There are fields so vast and remote that you can wander to their very centre and scream and bellow and laugh and dance, and much more besides, and no one but the mice and the crows will hear you.

There are fields that are near to nowhere, fields bigger than villages. Fields that feed hundreds of people and accommodate thousands of co-existing creatures and species, from the tiniest tick to the largest deer. Once, grey wolves and brown bears stalked the shrinking copses that grow at their fringes and then tentatively stepped out into the open fields too, but no more; the threat of their size meant they were hunted to extinction long ago.

And there are fields full of stories, century upon century of stories laid over one another, just as the bones of those who once turned and tilled the land and cultivated and harvested the crops, and shared their stories too, now lie rotting deep in the rich soil of a singular cemetery called England.

Into these fields reach the roots of an island. They reach and cling for meaning, for understanding. They are part of the story that has no ending.

Because the fields belong to everyone equally – past, present and future.

And out in the fields on a still summer's night, when the sky is an upturned mirror and the young crops harbour legions of creatures awaiting the totality of the moon's instruction, a light breeze lifts, causing a sea of platinum needles to shimmer, and strange things happen.

ALTON KELLETT
PATHWAY

On this particular night the moon is a signet ring held in soft wax and pressed to the black page of the sullen sky.

On the signet ring is a face, a fat face, the face of the moon, with the butterball cheeks of a cherub. It purses its pale lips and from high up above offers an enigmatic smile upon the field of incipient wheat.

One of the men stands looking at it for a lingering moment and tries to remember the names given to the different maria – those wide areas of the moon that look like seas, but which are in fact vast waterless plains of molten rock. The Sea of Tranquillity is the one most people know. But there are more, many more, and together they form a type of poetry centred around the theme of deep and unending desolation.

The Sea of Fecundity. The Sea of Cleverness.

The Sea of Crises. The Sea of Nectar.

He whispers the words just loud enough for them to become real. He wraps his tongue around them, and they become poetry in his mouth.

There are, of course, he thinks, the other features of the moon's surface too, such as its mountains and valleys, its craters, marshes and bays. As a boy he knew the names of so many of these different topographical lunar elements, and in fact kept a notebook in which he jotted them down each time he learned a new one.

The Bay of Rainbows. The Marsh of Sleep.

The Land of Sterility.

The Lake of Death.

Licking dirt-dry lips, he repeats them to himself now in a coarse whisper.

There were the names of the constellations too, all but the most obvious of which are now forgotten, for time has passed and his memory has become preoccupied with other things, like the names of girls and songs, and snatched recollections of people and places and parties. New memories have replaced old ones; memories of long warm days of endless potential and the occasional dire night folded shivering and slowly sobering in a police cell. His mind is cluttered with recollections of rhapsodic birdsong and paintings he has done and rivers he has swum; it is a photograph album containing fading pictures of roadsides he has parked up by and made a home from, and woodlands he has wandered, and also made a home from. There are images of bonfires and bottles of home brew in there. People and places, friends and faces. Long nights filled with laughter and fleeting scenes of what at the time felt like a form of madness, and surely was.

As a younger man – before he knew himself better – he went through a phase of walking around the village in a cape with the image of a large eyeball stitched upon it. Several of his haircuts were legendary. These are the thoughts that replace the names he carefully wrote down and which are consigned to an old notebook long since lost.

He remembers the bad things too: fist fights and heartbreak, broken bottles, swinging truncheons and a litany of injustices. He remembers all that. As a boy his daydreaming mind was a nest of twinkling trinkets, and though recent memories continue to replace old ones, each day bringing a new delivery of things to be processed, the strongest and most significant endure.

His name is Redbone.

Sensing a distance growing behind him, the other man, whose name is Calvert, stops and turns back to face his friend, who he sees, not for the first time, is standing waist-deep in the young crop, gazing at the cloudless firmament. He allows him half a minute and then gives a short, sharp whistle so accurately delivered that it is as perfect a part of the settling night's soundtrack as an owl hoot or the curdling screech of distant mating foxes. It is practised, a sound that belongs. It fits flush into the jigsaw puzzle of their endeavour.

Calvert is wearing sunglasses. The lenses are as dark as burned-out stars drifting through infinite time and space, vortices of nothingness.

A brief flash of white light – the same flash that preceded an explosion that was so sudden and so loud he still hears it now, years later, in the wind and sirens and the slamming of car doors and ice cream van music, even in the laughter of carefree children running down the street on uncertain legs – has left him with ocular sensitivity. The sunglasses never leave his face, even at night.

They hide the truth of a person, and he likes that too.

Redbone often thinks that were his friend to remove his sunglasses there would be another pair of sunglasses underneath, and then beneath those a third pair, with some eyes painted onto them.

Beneath that, who knows.

Were he asked, Calvert might reply that he sees and feels life as a slug, a seagull or a sheep might: it is simply something that is happening now. Existence is simply there, like a lightbulb or a downpour, until it isn't, experience occurs until it doesn't, and the dark-tint of his reality is precisely that: *his*. There are reasons he feels this way. Very specific reasons.

Moonstruck and drifting through memory, at the sound of the whistle Redbone comes back into being with a turning of an unwashed head, and he sees Calvert and then continues to walk slowly towards him. He moves in no hurry; he rarely does. He likes to let the globe move beneath his feet and do the work for him.

Though keen to press on, Calvert, whose natural pace in all areas of his life is a strident and purposeful march, waits for him.

In the milk-coloured lunar light Redbone looks at his friend as he approaches him and sees the streak of scarring that runs like an exposed bone along his jawline, then up into a tightly twisted knot of tissue across his cheek and underneath one shaded lens, to just beneath his hidden eye. Tonight it appears lustrously silver; ornate and baroque, almost, as exotic as the surface of the moon itself. It makes Redbone think of the theatrical half-mask worn by a character in a musical he has never seen.

Calvert also wears a beard. The block of ragged hair that hangs like a bib is another obstacle, a barrier, a hurdle that the world must climb over or look beyond in order to reach the man beneath it. The beard is so big and so thick that it appears as if it might be on loan from the props department of a film about gold prospectors and trappers sporting beaver-skin hats.

The beard is so big and so thick that Calvert's nose looks like a featherless newborn bird in the nest of his face, or perhaps a dormant penis.

Together with the sunglasses it makes for a formidable and near impenetrable visual combination, as if Calvert were a man in search of a motorcycle that he parked three days ago.

His is a face that could win poker tournaments.

Redbone does not recall his friend without the scar, without the sunglasses, without the beard; they are all as much a part of him as the unspoken traumas that only very occasionally flash like that brief burst of white light in the wet blackness of his hidden eyes. For Calvert is a human cactus, spiky and self-contained. He draws upon a deep well of resources.

O

Calvert carries the big post over one shoulder and the longer coil of rope over the other while Redbone has the short planks and the battered old bait bag containing tent pegs, headtorches, batteries, biscuits, apples, water.

When his friend has nearly reached him, Calvert continues along what remains of a tractor path that runs through the wheat crop. There is still a slight chill in the air but he is glad that the ground is dry. If they tread lightly they will leave no footprints. This is important. They will leave no trace.

Winter is forgotten now and spring is advancing at speed, while summer lurks not far beyond the swollen moment, a cold-blooded lizard-skinned beast sitting deep in the ancient dust of an ancient island. Soon it will waken.

As they follow the gentle decline down towards what they perceive to be the centre of this great sloping plain of crops, Redbone runs his free hand across the top of the wheat and feels the adolescent green bristles tickle his rough palms. They are as coarse as horsehair, as long as a feral cat's whiskers. He takes a head between thumb and forefinger and plucks it in a twisting motion. The grain has a budding stiffness to it as he grinds it in his hand, his palm acting as both fleshy pestle and clammy mortar, yet it holds its shape. No seeds come loose. Patiently awaiting long unbroken bursts of sunshine to give it life, the head of wheat is still in the early days of cultivation and has not yet reached its ultimate form. For now the produce is sun-starved and has a whole season ahead of it, as do the men. It is still green, as are the men.

Calvert walks briskly and with purpose. Two slow dark seasons of planning in quiet and cramped domestic anticipation in front of a fire have made him more focused than ever, and he is doing his best not to let his impatience overwhelm the task at hand. It is a trait that made him so effective in the Forces, yet which occasionally set him at odds with the rest of the team.

Redbone is still expected to keep pace and has long since learned that to protest against it is futile.

Suddenly Calvert stops and raises a hand. A military signal. Twenty paces behind him, Redbone stops too.

Calvert drops to a crouch in the crop.

Redbone does too.

They wait like this in the stone-grit silence for a full minute, then two. Except the night isn't entirely silent – it isn't silent at all – because in their motionless moments they both tune in to the sounds around them just as they did when they were children tuning in to radios held steady beneath the hot-breath darkness of their duvets. Close by they can detect the rustling and skittering of industrious creatures at work – field mice, mainly, though they know that hedgehogs, badgers, rabbits and hares are out here too.

And foxes, certainly, each night sneaking to snatch a rabbit or raid a chicken coop on one of the many old farms that demarcate the different acreages, and whose names Calvert has come to learn by rote during his winter's forensic research. Places like Leighton Latimer, Grey Bull Pastures or the wonderfully droll Hill End Hill.

The slightest breeze runs through the heads of wheat again; later in the season they will rattle like percussion, but for now they still carry within them moisture rising from the soil through the nodal cavities of the lower parts of their stalks, so it is a softer, greener breeze that the two men hear as it wends through the burgeoning crop. Each young green head is sticky to the touch. These are their salad days.

Somewhere far above can be heard the afterthought of an aeroplane embarking upon a night flight to a faraway country, another land, a land overseas, with its own crops and creatures, its own strange men with their own strange ways.

Calvert turns his head to Redbone, nods, and then they slowly stand. Two curled fingers intimate that they should continue onwards, so Redbone shifts the bag on his back and readjusts the short planks, and then follows his friend as he continues to silently recite the names of the areas of the moon left long behind him in the swirling litter of childhood memory.

O

Alton Kellett is a twenty-mile drive across the county line, almost exactly due south-west from the village in which they both live.

It was still light when Redbone picked Calvert up in his VW van from outside The Feathers an hour or two ago, just as he had before every mission last summer, and the summer before that too. 'Mission' is a word that Calvert favours, for it implies purpose, intent, and an element of intrigue.

Seeing Redbone, he slowly stood, straightened, then waggled first one leg and then the other in an attempt to shake off the pain of bone spurs that he'd sustained in a crush injury during an Air Troop training jump in Kenya, unwisely executed into a drop zone at high altitude and in stifling humidity. On damp days in endless English autumns he feels the knotted lumps of bone stiff in his joints, but even now, after sitting for a while in the dropping sun, the ache of past adventures had set in.

He stretched his arms as the sun sank low beyond the same hill on which they'd played as boys.

His heart too sank slightly at the sight of Redbone's van as it coughed its way round the war memorial and stalled with an uncertain judder in front of him. At the last count it had 140,000 miles on its clock and appeared to be comprised of parts from different vehicles either gifted to him or found in scrapyards – a rust-coloured wing here, a mismatched tyre there – to such an extent that it was now on the verge of being a different vehicle entirely. 'Like a past-it group that steadily replaces all its dying members, but still keeps touring under the same name,' was how Redbone once proudly described it. Yet somehow it continues to defy the automobile gods by not only running after all those miles, but also frequently providing a sometime home to Redbone, whenever he has the urge to go roaming for a few days or weeks, or has been kicked out by whichever woman he happens to be cohabiting with.

'First one of the year,' he said as his friend climbed in.

Redbone's words hung there between them like something solid, an obstruction.

'Best to start gently,' replied Calvert, the more pragmatic of the two.

'Yes.'

'Dust off the rust. Pace ourselves.'

'Pace the people, more like,' said Redbone. 'The public, I mean. They won't know what's hit them. Too much beauty can be damaging.'

'We'll ease into it,' remarked Calvert.

Redbone started the engine and they drove on into the last burning orange crescent of the skulking sun.

O

Redbone and Calvert met ten years ago, or perhaps it was twenty or fifty or six thousand years ago because the fact is the details of the past do not matter much to either of them. They do not fill their heads with significant dates or nostalgic shared recollections. They are not those kind of men. Neither has been stricken with the ailment known as sentimentality.

While Redbone is the more fanciful of the two he does not let this character trait define him, though he does have a weak spot for animals; the thought of a stray dog, an orphan goat or an ill-treated donkey can rapidly unravel him, and he has been known to wade out up to his neck into stagnant ponds to save drowning flies. Despite his past profession, Calvert meanwhile is not quite the warrior who should be given a wide pavement berth by passing strangers, as some might initially assume from his outward appearance. His quiet anxieties are legion. Deep waters run within him and strange creatures dwell down there in the darkness. Frequent are the days when he feels anxiety stretched tight over everything like clingfilm, and so for reasons as different as black and white or wrong and right, both men choose to exist mainly in the present moment. That they arrived at this point from different directions, but at a similar time in their eventful lives, is what binds them together. Similarly, having come to the understanding that life is just a brief phase on time's hyperbolic continuum, and that there have been other lives, and there will be other lives again, there are few things either of them truly care about, but making crop circles is one of them.

Sometimes it feels like it is the *only* thing.

O

It was part-dark when they parked up a mile or so from the tract of their choosing.

They set off for the field and the deep unending expanse of time and space enshrouded them. The south-west rolled away beyond the limits of their restricted vision, but the knowledge that beasts and birds were secreting themselves in the folds of the land, and would come to no harm by their hand, gave them comfort.

Beyond the existence of the crops themselves, out here all signs of modern civilisation were nowhere to be seen. There was only the night, the moment, and new mythologies waiting to be spun.

'Torches off,' said Calvert as they cleared a stile and tramped the first field.

And now, after much stargazing and dawdling on Redbone's part and self-restraint on Calvert's, the two men reach their chosen point of origin for their first design of the season, a circle-within-a-circle pattern accompanied by a pair of precise adjacent stripes known as pathways running on either side.

They call it the Alton Kellett Pathway.

When they have settled on a spot they take their lengths of rope and feed them through two holes at either end of the planks that they will place underfoot in order to flatten the crop. They use the longer rope as a radial line to map out the circle's perimeter. This Calvert does by having Redbone tie the rope around his torso for him, tucked into his armpits. When this is done the latter takes a long swig of water from a chipped green metal military flask, licks his lips, and then takes some more. His face is only half visible to Calvert when he speaks.

'It feels good to be back, though, doesn't it. Back in the game. Back in the field.'

'Oh yes,' says Calvert. 'Yes indeed.'

'I think this will be our summer.'

'I think so too.'

'A summer of glory.'

'As long as we stick to the code.'

The code does not need repeating. Redbone already knows that the code represents a strict set of rules that the pair have adhered to for the past two summers, back when their long-term venture began out of necessity, folly, anxiety, impish disruption and much more besides.

The code includes several non-negotiable, mutually agreed-upon rules. These include: parking at least a mile from whichever field they have chosen to work in; never visiting a location twice – not even days or weeks later; consistently destroying any written plans, designs or other material that might potentially be used as evidence against them (most commonly hastily folded into Calvert's wood-burning stove); keeping the VW fully taxed and insured (as the owner this is Redbone's job, though knowing his friend's lackadaisical attitude in most areas of his life, not to mention his complete distrust of all forms of authority and bureaucracy, Calvert asks him about it frequently); never being intoxicated beyond a pint or two (teetotal for several years, this does not apply to Calvert); never carrying anything that could accidentally start a fire (fuel, matches, lighters and so forth); never willingly damaging or destroying either a crop or a landowner's property or, indeed, unduly disturbing any living animal's natural habitat; refuting violence and avoiding confrontation whenever possible; refusing all comment if arrested; never publicly challenging inane conspiracies about the origin of crop circles lest it draw attention to their insider's knowledge of the subject; continually striving towards beauty; and, most importantly, never telling another soul about their endeavour. This is the one rule above all others.

'Always,' says Redbone, when Calvert repeats it now. '*All ways.*'

'Because our power lies in our secrecy. Our anonymity.'

'I know.'

'Without it, the mystery crumbles like a sandcastle. And the mystery is everything.'

'I *know*.'

'Even when some conspiracy theory nut-job is mouthing off in The Feathers about aliens – '

'*Especially* when some conspiracy theory nut-job is mouthing off in The Feathers about aliens,' interjects Redbone. 'Fuel the myth and strive for beauty, yes, but never reveal the truth.'

'Fuel the myth and strive for beauty' is another phrase that Redbone often repeats, as his one prevailing ambition in life (other than the slightly nebulous concept of continually 'sticking it' to 'The Man' who he views as being responsible for global spiritual decline) is to achieve the status of the mythical. This will, he hopes, be achieved through the increasingly intricate crop circle designs that he conceives, sometimes during a heightened state of consciousness, and which the pair of them then carefully execute under Calvert's direction as an experienced man of many years of combat in multiple terrains far more hostile than a gentle field on a pleasant summer's night.

For both of them, at different points, life has felt like a rope bridge over a narrow but bottomless chasm, with fine strands having already frayed and snapped. Crop circling provides a lifeline.

Life has a limit and it is not the *notorious* or the *infamous* to which Redbone strives but the mythical, which is something else entirely. This is important. At first he craved his name becoming one that people might raise a toast to over nut-brown pints in wood-panelled pub snugs and back rooms in the many decades, or centuries even, to come, someone whose deeds would be spoken about in reverential and incredulous tones, and maybe even written about in books or captured in song.

'Achieving the status of folk mythology, and being remembered as a revered outlaw amongst my own people,' he once said during the pair's first summer of fieldwork. 'What could be better?'

'An impossibility,' replied Calvert without hesitation. 'Our names can never be known. That's the whole point of all this.'

Out of this exchange came their code of conduct, always recited and remembered rather than written down. And now, several dozen crop formations later, Redbone is no longer so concerned with achieving the status of an indigenous outlaw folk hero, and instead has slowly learned to reconcile the beautiful irony of such an impossible ambition: that his name can never be revealed, at least not in his lifetime. Unlike his friend Calvert, who emphatically revels in the secrecy of it all, this has taken a long time to accept. Now, as they embark upon their third summer of mischief and glory-seeking, he finally accepts that the power of the crop circles they have made, and will make this summer, lies in their growing ability to inspire such questions as *who?* and *how?* and, perhaps to an even greater extent: *why?*

The absence of fame and a need for complete anonymity does not, however, prevent Redbone from elevating himself into a mythical being in the quieter moments of his own febrile imagination, a folkloric figure sent to mess with the minds of the suburban starched-collar straights and the buttoned-down norms. And while his motivation is one of a prankster's intentional confusion, it is an aesthetic pursuit too: fuel the myth, yes. But strive for beauty, always.

Also Redbone has little choice in the matter. The code of silence that Calvert has imposed upon him has now become mafia-like in its resolve, an *omertà* of the grassy downs and chalk plains, as they wade waist-deep in the wheat, oat and barley crops of an England that in their minds is a kingdom that belongs entirely to the dreaming dissenters and the rat-tailed revolutionaries, and is open to all-comers. All borders and boundaries, whether visible or not, are only there for the burning.

O

Calvert has his own reasons for embarking upon these night raids. Though it has not been verbalised, Redbone knows that these long missions in the fields are therapeutic for his friend. They provide focus for a mind racked by those things seen and heard, tasted and smelled in the arena of conflict. Out here the horrors he has witnessed are forgotten for a while at least.

Beauty for beauty's sake, and the sense of pride that they instil in their covert work, are the two points upon which they both agree.

To create something that beguiles and baffles, that thrills and confuses – to create something so stunning and arresting and *sudden* – something sprung from the earth like a dawn mushroom, a gift to the people, is, they both reason, a radical and benevolent act of the purest and highest order.

And from such pure intentions myths are made.

O

So they separate and they create.

The two men tread the young crop flat in such a way that not a single stalk is broken. With pegged ropes as their guide, they circle a fulcrum and push their short planks down with just enough pressure to make a mark. A narrow circumference path slowly wheels its way around an unseen centre like a tiny miracle.

They do not speak.

They do not need to, for they are working in perfect silent symbiosis, each man wordless as he fulfils his allotted task according to a predetermined plan which, if stuck to rigidly, will yield the desired results, just as the farmer yields his bountiful crop by following centuries-old practices that are hewn from experience.

The pattern grows and they have to use their imaginations as to how it might look from above. Down here it feels rough, a little ragged around the edges, but past endeavours have taught them otherwise; down here fine details get lost in the immensity of their designs, and matter little. The sky is their intended audience. The bigger picture is the only picture.

Though it is Redbone's imagination that conceives of the crop circles – the pair having long since reconciled themselves to the inadequacy of this term, which is now being used internationally to describe concoctions that are way beyond simple wheel-like designs – it is Calvert, a veteran of hundreds of freefall parachute jumps, who is better at visualising them from the air; ten years of training taught him focus, gave him a finely tuned sense of perspective, and literally broadened his horizon.

If the former thinks the latter's line is not true, which is a rarity, he puts down his planks and walks over to help set him on the right track, or if Calvert thinks his friend is too slow, or too noisy, or dangerously distracted, he does the same. Otherwise they work alone yet together, pausing only to survey the land around them and to drink water, which they do now in silence as Redbone cranes his neck to stare at the moon once more and Calvert studies the plan which by morning will be burned.

The first of the season.

Without warning, their work is suddenly disturbed by a noise at the far end of the field, that of a gate clattering open, followed by the pneumatic hiss of brakes being applied. It is a most unwanted intrusion just as it feels as if the modern world is beginning to slip away.

Though they are close to a hundred yards apart, both men immediately stop and instinctively duck to a crouch, as alert as animals. They wait like this for a full minute, but then there is another noise: voices, and then a mechanical sound. It is the grind of hydraulics as the back of a truck is raised, followed by the slide and clatter of something, or some *things*, being deposited. A cacophony of household waste. Junk and detritus.

The refuse falls onto the earth, crunching the edge of the crop.

Calvert raises his head above the green crown of the nascent wheat. He sees the rear lights of a truck flashing red in the dark, like the eyes of an oversized owl or an adder caught in a torch beam. A malevolent glare. Further light from the truck's cab casts a small half-circle around the front of the vehicle, and he sees that there are at least two men there. They are far away, but the stillness of the night carries their voices. It amplifies them so that they dominate the space around them.

Redbone raises his head too. He sees the same scene and then looks across to where he thinks Calvert is, but he cannot see him. Calvert briefly worries that his friend, always impulsive, might voice his objections, as he himself wishes he could.

But he knows they cannot do this, for that would be to reveal themselves, and that could jeopardise their entire endeavour – and not just tonight either, but the entire summer ahead, and all the summers yet to come.

Instead they squat, watching.

Watching and waiting.

Waiting, with anger rising.

The truck pulls away from the field and they see the red lights fade from view. Only then do they stand and walk down towards the far end of the field, their walk becoming a hurried jog as they arrive almost at the same time to see a dumped mass of rubbish. As they move closer they see that it contains a freezer, office chairs, carrier bags containing unidentified contents, VHS cassettes of children's cartoons, old shoes, a knotted duvet, empty plastic crates, soiled nappies, a broken lamp, many green lager bottles – dozens and dozens of them – some roofing felt, a large roll of carpet, gas canisters from a SodaStream, several hundred broken bricks with chunks of cement still attached to them, a pair of roller boots, a length of drainpipe, a wadded lump of rain-soiled magazines and a plastic pink garden slide. In the moonlight the fly-tipped mound has a heightened, almost absurd and unreal quality to it. It is a small mountain, a totem to consumerism, contemporary domesticity and indiscriminate disposability.

'Bastards,' says Calvert.

'Not a single thing in it that will decompose,' replies Redbone, melancholy souring his tone like vinegar tipped into a cocktail.

'Bastards.'

'Not a thing.'

'Apart from the paper. But still: bastards.'

They kick at the rubbish. They toe it, shaking their heads and saying little.

'How can people do that?' says Redbone. 'Some of this will be here for centuries if it doesn't get moved.'

Calvert doesn't reply at first, then he quietly says: 'I'd like to chop their hands off.'

'On our patch as well, Ivan,' says Redbone. 'On our canvas. They've not even bothered to close the gate behind them. We should have a rummage. There might be bills in there, or receipts that identify the culprits. Incriminating letters. We should have a rummage to see what we can find.'

Calvert shakes his head. 'We can't risk it.'

They stand saying nothing because there is nothing that can be said that is as demonstrative and definitive as prolonged silence rounded off by several curt tuts of exasperation and deep sighs of resignation.

Finally Redbone speaks. 'How far off finishing up do you reckon we are?'

Calvert scratches his chin. 'I don't know. An hour, tops?'

'We should get it done, then.'

'Agreed. We need to get out of here in case someone pins this on us.'

They silently turn away and walk back into the green field.

○

Dawn breaks like a dropped bottle of something sweet and sticky, but for an hour or so the outlying hills remain charcoal smears as rough as the grain of a sugar paper sky. The sky has a scent. The scent of potential. A new day. New hope.

Anger at the fly-tipping has urged the two men on. It is not only anger at the thoughtlessness and arrogance of the people who did this, but also anger because the purity and perfection of the virginal spring night has been tainted by a flagrant attack on the landscape they love so much. And therefore it is an attack on them.

The outside world has intruded upon these moments that both men have been dreaming about for many months.

With their heads containing a rattle-bag of complex and conflicting emotions, they leave on weary legs, their debut artwork of the season complete.

A mysterious pattern has appeared overnight in a wheat field near Alton Kellett. The design is the first local sighting of the growing phenomenon known as 'crop circles', whose origins and creators are the subject of much speculation. Many believe them to be the result of paranormal activity. Whoever – or whatever – embarked upon this act of trespass and vandalism is also believed to be responsible for a substantial amount of household waste that was illegally dumped in an adjacent field, at significant cost to taxpayers.

Alton Kellett Parish
Weekly News Sheet,
1 June 1989

WHITE WHATTLE KEYS

'Did you see it?'

Redbone asks the question before Calvert has had time to hoist himself up into the VW that his friend has haphazardly parked by the old wooden bench outside The Feathers.

The bench is weather-worn and a little bit warped. One of its legs is shorter than the other three so that it wobbles whenever he sits down on it, though time has taught Calvert the correct end at which to place himself to avoid this happening. There is a plaque attached to the bench. The plaque says:

Uriah Greenman

1890–1979

Dum spiro spero

Calvert always wondered what the phrase meant until one day the wondering became too insistent to ignore and he walked to the library and looked it up. He discovered that it means 'While I breathe, I hope', and now he uses the phrase as a mantra whenever life feels as if it is becoming a looming grey cliff face of sheer and slippery rock of insurmountable magnitude. '*Dum spiro spero*,' he mutters quietly to himself in the long and lonely sleepless winter hours spent staring into the glowing coals of his fire. '*Dum spiro spero*,' he mutters when some unseen force appears to prevent him crossing the threshold of his house and stepping out into the street to complete a mundane task. '*Dum spiro spero*,' he mutters when he finds himself watching a television that has not been turned on.

When he does not answer, Redbone asks him the question again: 'I said, "Did you see it?"'

Calvert looks around and then gets in the van. He is hit by the familiar smell of stale tobacco smoke and deep-set damp, of earth and unwashed bodies. Once, he found a bird's nest in the corner of the ceiling of Redbone's van, where a family of wrens had made a home for themselves over one winter. Redbone claimed not to have noticed it amongst the mussed mess of cables, camping equipment, battered bass guitars, blankets, amplifiers, empty cans and plastic jugs, tools, a ladder, rope, mouldy books, kindling and old army boots still caked with mud from a forgotten festival, though he did not appear unduly surprised when Calvert pointed it out to him. He even left one window open so that the tiny darting birds could come and go as they pleased, and occasionally brought them writhing worms and maggots left over from fishing trips.

'Yes,' he says, after a long pause. 'I saw it.'

'What did you think?'

'It looked decent,' says Calvert.

Redbone starts the engine and lets it tick over for a moment.

'Only decent?'

'The pathways were a bit off. A bit wonky.'

Redbone frowns but he doesn't disagree because he knows that this judgement is correct.

'But,' says Calvert, 'it was not bad for the first one of the summer. Our debut. We just need to blow away the cobwebs.'

'Page four of the local newsletter. I mean, it has a small circulation, but still. And as you say, it's the first of the summer.'

'We'll do better. And the better they are, the more people will notice.'

'Build it and they will come.'

'Exactly. *Dum spiro spero.*'

'What?'

'It doesn't matter.'

'Well, anyway,' says Redbone as he reaches into the glove compartment and takes out a roll of paper, 'check this out.'

'Not here. Let's drive a bit first. You never know who is passing.'

Redbone places the design he has drawn for the evening back in the glove compartment, and then pulls away from the square. Within a few minutes they are rattling down narrow lanes towards the hamlet of White Whattle.

As they pause at a junction for a moment they hear the call of the cuckoo, the sonorous song of it, sung from little lungs, a sweet thrum freed from the funnel of its throat. It is a call down the centuries, shaped by deep time and desire. Desire to spread the message that summer is coming in on the breeze and all the sins of winter shall be forgiven and forgotten. Forgotten as the new scents and notes stir senses nullified by dead seasons past.

And the first sound of the burgeoning summer is this call of the cuckoo, an echo from a distant copse, a canticle for the warming land. Unseen others join it in a choral round, their stout, sculpted beaks opening and closing, almost mechanically, to sup the sun, and the cuckoo's song sings on.

The two men's ears receive it with gratitude.

O

White Whattle is a hamlet only in name, and is in fact more of a scattering of houses constructed for the workers on a large dairy farm around which they congregate and after which the place is named. They are not idyllic cottages, but functional red-brick houses built just after World War II. They each have small front and back gardens, originally used for the growing of vegetables during the lean post-war times, and then directly behind them are flat grass meadows, fenced off into manageable uniform shapes whose old boundaries, still visible in their ancient hedgerows, go back to the days of enclosure; used in rotation, these are for the grazing of cattle. There are trampolines in their gardens and bicycles dumped haphazardly in the growing grass. Further off in the distance the old tilled and turned arable land of Redbone and Calvert's ancestors gives way to more recently cultivated agricultural fields thick with wheat and barley crops being intensively grown on a mass scale.

Only two of the cottages are occupied by herdsmen and their families now; the others are privately rented. Calvert knows this because he consulted the electoral roll in the library one afternoon last winter. He did the same for most of this season's locations, checking to see if any police, judges, barristers, magistrates, MPs, lawyers or other notable figureheads of establishment institutions lived close by, for it was they who were more likely to give them grief if they happened to be interrupted or apprehended. In this case Redbone, whose distaste for establishment figures is even more vocal due to a litany of minor charges – trespass, possession, noise pollution, avoidance of fines, and so forth – acquiesced with his friend's fastidiousness.

'Torches off,' says Calvert as they approach the houses and then pass by them to follow the curving road between the velvet drapes of nightfall. They vault a fence and then make their way across a large field of cows. The sleepy beasts, emancipated from their straw-laden winter sheds where a cruel winter wind blew across the concrete forecourt, detect their presence in the muted murkiness, and in return the men hear the shifting and snorting sounds of the strong shorthorn milkers as they settle in for the night.

Then they hear something behind them. It is less a snort and more a gruff, agitated sigh, followed by the sound of dirt being hacked at and stamped.

Calvert swings round first.

'Bull,' he says.

'What?' says Redbone, but he does not need an answer, for as he too turns he sees a russet-coloured beast facing them from fifty paces in the gloom. There is no fence between them, and its neck and shoulders are wide in a way that makes Redbone think of the rugby players who, for reasons unknown, choose to gather in The Feathers on a Sunday evening to sing their bawdy songs, partake in mindless drinking contests and pull each other's trousers down, before heading back to the towns and cities in the morning where they work as property developers, bankers and financiers, and other jobs that enable them to own cars that loudly advertise their sense of entitlement.

Calvert glances to his right. He checks the far perimeter fence.

'We'll keep walking that way. No sudden movements and stay close by. It's when there's heifers or calves around that they get lairy. Or if they're cornered.'

'Aye aye, Captain,' says Redbone, who appears surprisingly unfazed by the prospect that they might be flattened, tossed or skewered by a young bull weighing as much as a small automobile.

'He's still got his balls.'

'You can see them from here?'

'Yes,' says Calvert. 'You need twenty-twenty vision to serve in the Special Forces. Let's keep walking. Bulls that still have their stones are the ones you have to watch. If he charges we'll have to leg it and leap the perimeter fence.'

But the bull does not make a move. Instead he watches as the two men fade into the dim and distant haze of night, then sniffs the air and draws in the scent of the heifers in the next field that he fully intends to service at the first available opportunity.

O

They walk for half an hour until White Whattle is nothing but a few flickering pinprick lights, like stars that have fallen and are now perched on the camber of the land behind them. Out here there is nothing but a rising breeze in the barley that is as strong as the famed mistral that blows across southern France and into the northern waters of the Mediterranean. Welcomed, it cools the beads of sweat on their brows.

Behind him, Calvert hears a sort of chuckle, a short joyous hiss, like a shaken can of beer being opened. He turns to his friend, eyes him sideways. He's like a lizard, he thinks. Redbone is like a skink. A scrawny skink in an old camo jacket.

Not for the first time it strikes Calvert that he does not actually know his friend's real name, only that he is Redbone, a nick-name that, as far as Calvert is aware, he obtained in childhood, and which was probably arrived at, as so many nicknames are, by the most circuitous of routes. Too much time has passed for him to ask Redbone's real name now; their shared experiences out in the fields mean that to enquire would be not only awkward but also somewhat ludicrous. Who knows, maybe he really is called Redbone. Colin or Brian or Keith Redbone. Or perhaps it is something far more unexpected. An old Anglo-Saxon name, perhaps, like Hereward or Sigeberht or Wigmund. Ælfstan Redbone. Calvert affords himself a small smile at this idea.

The fact that he doesn't know his best friend's name also adds an element of secrecy to their operation, which is functionally comparable to both terrorist and counter-intelligence units, where information networks are often reduced to conjoined cells, each featuring as few as three members, with the rest of the matrix unknown to them. Calvert knows that were he to be captured and tortured he would not be able to give up his friend's name, even if he wanted to. The chance of this happening is, of course, somewhat unlikely, but reasoning that you never know what future regime changes might bring, and that all such skills and knowledge are transferable to unforeseen scenarios, Calvert still values a tried and tested fail-safe security measure such as this.

Redbone meanwhile knows that his partner's full name is Ivan Robin Calvert, not least because he has it tattooed on one fleshy bicep that is kept pumped up like a small football by a daily regime of free weights, alongside a strict routine of callisthenics, running and yoga, not to mention his eccentric diet. He also knows that the tattoo was done three days before Calvert was deployed to Ascension Island in the South Atlantic for last-minute training seven long springs ago; no explanation as to the motivations behind the tattoo was ever offered. The message was implicit: it served the purpose of a permanent toe-tag as he entered the chaos and confusion of conflict on a far-flung rock in a lonely ocean.

Around Calvert's name Redbone has also observed an older inking of a snake coiling the tanned ham-like flank of his upper arm. Calvert once confided that it represents an eighteenth-century antiquarian's theory that the scattering of ancient standing stones at nearby Avebury, a place beloved of both men, had in fact been carefully laid there by their prehistoric ancestors in the formation of a vast snake whose tail at Beckhampton Avenue led to the henge at Avebury, before then twisting along the West Kennet Avenue and to the head at an area known as the Sanctuary. It is a theory Calvert once tested from the peak of the mysterious chalk burial mound of nearby Silbury Hill, atop which he also once revealed to Redbone in a rare moment of openness and quiet sincerity that he was aggressively sucked off as a teenager by an intimidating biker called Carol who had oversized protruding eyes and, sloshing with cloudy cider, drove him home afterwards, helmetless and pillion, down the winding country lanes at great speed.

The inked serpent, now fading after more than a decade and several journeys through vastly differing climates, reminds Calvert of a happier, more simple time, not long before he undertook the arduous selection training for the Special Air Service during five particularly cruel winter weeks in the Brecon Beacons.

It doesn't matter to Calvert that Redbone knows his full name as he is aware that his friend would last about twenty seconds under interrogation, and would swiftly reveal other key details that would surely lead interested parties to Calvert's door anyway. You'd only have to deny him a cigarette and he'd crack. He does not share such thoughts with Redbone, though, and never has.

He looks at his friend now for a long moment. In turn, Redbone sees the moon reflected in the jet-black plastic of Calvert's sunglasses. He also sees himself.

'Are you on something?' Calvert asks.

'I'm on a planet called earth,' says Redbone in a voice that he hopes is steady and measured.

'Hmmm,' replies Calvert, the short guttural noise weighted with scepticism.

Redbone tips his head back to the sky, to the stars, and issues a small, almost childlike sigh of wonderment.

'You're tripping, aren't you?'

'In a way,' says Redbone, his voice now distant and tiny in his throat, which he clears, and then tries again. 'In a way we're all tripping.'

'Yes, but in another very real way, we're definitely not.'

Redbone pulls his eyes away from the celestial display and looks at Calvert. He looks right through him and beams a sloppy, lopsided, cheek-chewing smile.

'OK, I'm *a bit* tripping.'

Calvert sighs.

'You're off your nut.'

'I'm not. I'm really not. In fact, I'm very much on my nut, and clinging to it most securely.'

'Mushrooms?'

'Mushrooms,' says Redbone. 'God's own sweeties.'

'How many?'

'I think the pertinent question here is: how strong?'

'Fine, then. How strong?'

'Ask me in twenty minutes or several earthly aeons rendered in phantasmagorical hues.'

Calvert shakes his head. 'Christ, you're a plank.'

'A plank serves many purposes.' Here he lifts the length of wood he has been carrying. 'See?'

'But you're high all the same.'

Redbone considers the statement. He gives it serious consideration.

'Well, yes. It's fair to say I'm gently hovering about six inches above the ground.'

'Oh, great. Just wonderful.'

'At least it's better than six feet under it.'

'But I thought we agreed no narcotics when we're conducting fieldwork,' says Calvert.

'Did we?'

'Yes. Last summer. It's a key part of the code, which you appear to have already forgotten.'

'Right,' says Redbone. 'See, I assumed those rules specifically applied to last summer's night ops only.'

'And *I* assumed a rule is not restricted by the calendar, and therefore it would carry over to this year's work too. I'm sure we discussed this last time.'

'Ah. Mixed wires, then. Crossed signals.'

'I'm not having a go at you,' says Calvert. 'It's just we're only on the second circle of the summer and I think you should save the tripping for when you're planning new designs, that's all. That way our endeavour might benefit from some practical application of your hallucinogenic explorations, rather than being hindered by them.'

'Is it the hovering that bothers you?'

'It might if you actually were. But you're not.'

'If it's any consolation, I believe that this particular dose was not only sourced last year, but came from very near here. The hill over yonder, in fact, carefully picked from piss-covered cowpats.'

'It's scant consolation,' says Calvert.

Undeterred, Redbone continues. 'So, in a way, the mushrooms come from this very land to feed the willing mind, which then in turn feeds the land via our wonderful creations, so to speak. It's a multi-dimensional food chain, the cycle of life, death and creation itself all taking place within several small acres of these rich fields and cow-covered hills. That's localism. That's community. No, wait, it's . . .'

Redbone's eyes widen with delight at his own emerging theory.

'It's *continuity*.'

Mild exasperation grappling with stifled amusement, Calvert shakes his head. He always finds it hard to get truly annoyed with his friend, and that is rare. Apart from one or two of the lads back in the regiment, pretty much everyone else he has encountered before or since has managed to rub him up the wrong way sooner or later. Redbone's charm is in his appetite for understanding this and an occasional naiveté not yet beaten out of him by life.

Redbone continues. 'Yes, I found them down the back of the radiator,' he says as much to himself as to his friend. 'I must have put them there to dry out last September at the circling season's end. They're quite weak, I think. And the moonlight.'

Calvert studies his friend once more.

'What about it?'

'The moonlight is refracted through the basket of my tongue.'

'Wow.'

O

Despite his friend's sarcasm – and the gentle rush of psilocybin that is flooding his system in mini-tsunamis of soil-spawned pleasure – Redbone can see that Calvert is in his element again. A sodden slate-grey autumn and washed-out winter stuck indoors were unkind to his friend, who appeared tense and pale when they first reconvened in the back snug of The Feathers to quietly finalise their summer plans. Being powerless to prevent the fly-tippers who polluted their space at Alton Kellett affected them both too, and set Calvert in particular off on the wrong foot.

Redbone knows that his friend is at his best doing fieldwork, and that too long alone with his thoughts and ruminations can have adverse effects, not only because Calvert is a field man as he is but also because he lives in what he claims is the second-smallest detached house in Britain.

Bluebell Cottage is a squat stone box of a building that has crouched near the centre of the village since it was built at the dawn of the eighteenth century. A doorway so small that even the shorter people of the early Georgian era would have stooped to get through leads straight from the street into a room that is only an inch or two over eight square feet, yet into which Calvert has miraculously managed to fit an L-shaped leather sofa whose covering is scored with thousands of scratch marks from his overzealous cat, Doorstep, as well as a drop-leaf table and a unit that houses his television and substantial videotape collection. A thick rag rug covers almost all of the uneven flagstone floor and a small inglenook fireplace holds within it the centrepiece of the room and Calvert's one other concession to modernity: a recently installed brand-new wood-burning stove. Around it, the stone of the fireplace is stained by over three centuries of soot and smoke, but Calvert keeps the green enamel of the wood burner buffed and shiny with regular cleaning.

Having never actually been invited in, Redbone has only ever stood in the diminutive doorway of Bluebell Cottage. Calvert's claim that it is simply too small to host two fully grown men for any length of time has always seemed reasonable enough, though he is fairly certain he understands why his friend really chooses to dwell in such a place: it reminds him of the many confined spaces in which he spent his formative years. Jeeps, cabins, helicopters, tanks and the like; places of trauma at certain times, but also places of comfort and familiarity at others.

A ladder to the left of the fireplace leads to a truncated platform loft space in which there is a mattress and a bookcase built from bricks and lengths of wood and which contains a small library of tomes primarily about war, combat, military history, strategic thinking, survival and food foraging, while many empty ginger ale bottles plugged with thumbs of spent candles are spaced around the perimeter. Calvert's clothes cling to hangers suspended on a length of rope strung across a room whose ceiling is too low to allow him to reach full height beneath it. At best he can only stand hunched like a garret-trapped golem.

The house is twelve feet and four inches in height from ground to the upstairs ceiling, two inches more than the 'so-called' smallest detached abode in Britain, one Thimble Hall in the Derbyshire Peaks. Calvert always prefaces mention of this place with 'so-called' as its status has never been verified by the *Guinness Book of World Records*, and pride in Bluebell Cottage makes him sceptical enough to frequently threaten to travel up to evaluate this miniature wonder with a tape measure of his own, though of course he never has, and almost certainly never will.

'My place used to house a family of eight,' he has remarked on several occasions, a claim made without evidence, and usually with an air of defensiveness.

A tiny extension out the back of his house holds a galley kitchen and a room in which there is a toilet and a shower so ineffective, and contained in so small a stall, that Calvert has to contort himself into all manner of positions in order to cleanse himself beneath a dribble whose flow is so weak as to appear comical.

His cooking is done on two rings and a tiny oven; there is space for neither fridge nor freezer. Here in his miniature abode Calvert has mastered the art of economy in both his lifestyle and his bodily movements, which, even when he is outside in the fields, remain measured, controlled. Minimum effort for maximum effect.

And Calvert does need to be outside. Now more than ever he feels the pull of the lanes, the meadows and the woods. Such a cramped domestic situation is only manageable if he can get out, and the drab and sunless winter starved him of purpose, so when the pair met at The Feathers on the eve of this season's debut mission, Redbone could see in his friend a burning desire to once more pursue this shared obsession.

O

On paper, tonight's formation resembles the cross section of an intricate lock.

'A lock awaiting the keys of daylight to open it to the world,' is how Redbone described it when he unveiled his design to Calvert after they'd parked down an obscure and unfamiliar lane that ended in a turning circle and padlocked metal gate. 'Isn't it something?'

The pattern features two large circles of differing sizes at either end of a main stem or spine, and from each of these circles, which also incorporate within them other smaller circles to create a target-like impression, extend claw shapes with teeth – or keys – that are inspired by the movable parts found in locks, clocks and other such mechanisms.

The design looks like a blueprint for a dormant machine, as if at any moment the wheels and cogs of it might start turning. Calvert had to admit, it was indeed *something*.

'I call it White Whattle Keys,' Redbone proudly announced. 'I did consider White Whattle Lock, but it sounded a little watery for my liking and we're a long way from canal country. Anyway, I've tailored it towards the young barley. A bespoke piece, you could say.'

And now they are bringing it to life on a grand scale as they walk their way in silence through the crop, circling back on themselves, pegging rope and carefully measuring angles against chosen land-marks. They work quickly, with daybreak snapping at their heels.

Just as the sky is shedding the burden of darkness to greet a new day, Redbone whistles to gain Calvert's attention, then gestures to a small bird that they have disturbed as it takes to the sky.

Calvert lays down his plank and walks towards him.

'What is it?'

'A corn bunting. Twitcher's nickname: the fat bird of the barley. Rare as anything. They're endangered. Practically extinct in Ireland.'

'I didn't see it,' says Calvert. 'Are you still tripping?'

'Monoculture,' says Redbone, ignoring his question. 'It's monoculture that is killing them off. Too much ploughing at the margins and over-trimming of hedges is leaving them without suitable feeding and breeding sites. Pesticides too, of course.'

Calvert nods in hushed agreement and lets his friend continue.

'The pesticides are killing off the weeds too, so that there are far less seeds and insects for them to feed on at this time of the year. They're mainly ground birds, you see, and all this oilseed rape crop that's being planted everywhere is too dense for birds like the corn bunting to nest in, and even if they do build nests then they and their chicks are threshed to ribbons by the machines come harvest. Poor little buggers.'

With the drug wearing off now and a fractured sense of melancholy setting in, Redbone sighs.

'A world without birds and birdsong will be a sad and lonely place.'

A local policeman has reported sighting an Unidentified Flying Object (UFO) at the weekend while on patrol. PC Keith Denny was returning from a call-out to a domestic incident at Newton Steeple when he claims to have seen a spaceship over the small hamlet of White Whattle in the southern part of the county at approximately 3 a.m. on Sunday morning.

'It was circular in shape and had flashing lights around its perimeter,' said PC Denny. 'The lights changed colour as it hovered at a height of approximately one hundred feet for a substantial amount of time before it accelerated away at great speed. I'm not normally a person prone to fanciful theories, but I am led to believe that the area received a visitation from alien entities, and that they meant us no harm.'

The sighting has been linked to an intricate crop circle that was discovered in farmland less than two miles east of White Whattle. The pattern, which was made by the flattening of wheat on a grand scale and features a series of 'key-like' shapes, was discovered by farmer Dick Collins. 'It just appeared overnight,' said Collins, 54. 'I am baffled as to who or what could have made it – and why. If it is aliens as this policeman suggests, then they respect farming, as not a single stalk of my crop has been snapped, which is more than I can say after we had some of those so-called "New Age" travellers here last year. Give it a week or two and it'll be right as rain again. It's certainly a mystery, though. My sheepdog went into premature labour the same day, and also an old grandfather clock in my kitchen stopped ticking after half a century.'

Wiltshire Times,
16 June 1989

TRAPPING ST EDMUNDS
SOLSTICE PENDULUM

21 June. Solstice, or midsummer, and everything feels elastic in the gloaming.

Air and land alike appear tightly wound and almost stretched to snapping point. All senses are heightened. The crop wavers mechanically like a forest of aerials. Around the two men the unseen creatures of the hundreds of acres are skittish and moon-drunk. High on their perches and clustered in the tangled hedgerows like wind-blown litter, the birds do not sleep. Cannot sleep. Tonight all living things are thin of skin and hot of blood.

Even the moon, always so passive and impartial an onlooker, is agitated.

Everything beneath it is alert. The land crackles and the nocturnal death drama plays on.

The two men are far apart, flattening the crop at the opposite ends of tonight's work, a design completed by Redbone only this afternoon. It is a sprawling masterpiece measuring nearly two hundred and fifty feet in length that they both agree shall be called the Trapping St Edmunds Solstice Pendulum.

The pattern is based around an elongated narrow central lane that incorporates three large circles along its length, the end ones of which are filled in and therefore require a huge amount of flattening, and also feature antennae protruding at precise angles, while the central circle requires less disruption to the wheat but does include two straight strips on either side of the central spine. Viewed from above, it takes the approximate shape of a particularly elaborate pendulum.

The drive out to Trapping St Edmunds took them forty minutes. The road was a ribbon from a spool being pushed about by a playful kitten and they parked too far from their intended canvas, so when they arrived shortly after sunset, they quickly began to regret the walk that stole precious minutes from the short time in which they had to work.

They already knew that the sun, *their* sun – the one that sits at the centre of the solar system – would rise again shortly before five so they swiftly walked towards the centre, and began working away from one another more quickly than they would have liked.

And now the acreage appears as vast as an ocean, a golden inland ocean that parts for them just as the lonely faraway waters of the South Atlantic might part for the hull of a destroyer as it glides into enemy waters. But out here the only conflicts are played out in the dust kingdom of the nocturnal questers.

The light tonight is strange and brilliant as Redbone and Calvert push through the crop. When they pause to listen to the sporadic concerto played by the unseen soloists of night – those fleet of foot and swift of wing – they become scarecrows guarding a lake of mercury. They hear the nocturne music that is entirely devoid of melody but not of meaning, for within it are animalistic expressions of hunger, fear, desire, all heightened by an instinctive awareness of the shortened night and the moon's radial power.

As a large cloud passes it becomes a liquid light, like molten metal pouring across the land. Far above the men, planets turn and blaze and burn, and below the imaginary meniscus of the placid crop, small mammals scuttle and scurry through the subterranean kingdom.

O

After three hours they allow themselves a short break. Redbone takes a drink. His throat is a Saharan sand dune, a dead riverbed of boulders. He is so thirsty that he swallows the water as if the lives of his unborn offspring depend upon it. He drains half the flask in a few greedy gulps so that non-existent children might one day live.

Squatting on his haunches, Calvert watches as a bee crawls curling out from a hole in the ground, shedding the absolute darkness of its early days. Nectar is in the air and though the bee is more solitary than most might realise, deep time has taught it to be intoxicated. Curious and a little confused, the bee takes flight to follow a sky map drawn from the senses and join a collective act of communion. Soon it will be promiscuous, drunk on desire and pollinating freely. A coating of toxic chemicals layered over the land around will send it further afield to purer patches and wilder spaces, if it can find any, and sweet shall be the ambrosia of the land that will sustain its short life. The flowers will open themselves, their petals peeling back like the pages of a pornographic book until the bee touches their insides. For now, its shape is caught in the glare of Calvert's torch.

'Look at that,' he says, but his friend is turned away from him, gazing at the moon. 'A bee, at night.'

'What?'

'Nothing,' he says quietly, glad to have the moment for himself.

In exchange for Redbone's work conceptualising each crop circle, Calvert's other task is to provide snacks. He likes to cook and considers himself a bold, resourceful and perhaps even pioneering culinary experimentalist who does not eschew palatability for sustenance's sake.

Since he left the Forces he has, however, abstained from eating meat. There was something about suffering serious flesh wounds, and the subsequent slow and painful recovery in which he watched his weeping flesh slowly knit back together beneath a thousand crusted dressings, that made the prospect of eating another creature feel too close to cannibalism. Suddenly the idea of meat being chewed and then sitting in his stomach was nothing short of repulsive. The spent life of another once-living thing inside him like that reminded him of cruelty, and cruelty reminded him of war, and war reminded him of so much more that he could not bear to face. Nevertheless he prides himself on possessing a daring palate and now creates his own vegetarian dishes, which he unpacks from two Tupperware boxes as they crouch in the crop.

'Here you are,' he says, passing one to Redbone.

'What is it?'

'Parsnip pyramids. They're Egyptian.'

'The parsnips?'

'No, the pyramids, you plum.'

Redbone lifts the lid and gingerly looks inside.

'It's mashed parsnip, shaped into pyramids, and then baked with a Parmesan sauce in the middle,' Calvert explains. 'In the central burial chamber, if you will.'

Redbone frowns. 'I'm not sure I will.'

'Be bold, man.'

Redbone lifts one out and takes a bite. It tastes like soft cold parsnip and strong gluey cheese that has congealed into one bogey-like string that dangles down his throat when he unsuccessfully tries to swallow it in one gulp. Yet still it is not his friend's worst effort and he is hungry, so he takes another bite.

'Thanks,' he says, looking over at Calvert, who is already pushing his third and final pyramid into his mouth in one go and chewing noisily while staring at the moon's grey penumbra.

'Some of the old faces are off to the 'Henge tonight,' says Redbone after he has managed to ingest one more of the tetrahedron-shaped root vegetable treats. 'It's party time, but they say there's going to be trouble.'

Redbone is one of those people who change their hairstyle on a weekly basis, or if not their hairstyle then the colour of it. It is as if the restless nature of his wandering and occasionally brilliant mind keeps sprouting out of his skull in a physical follicular expression that often causes small children to run after him, laughing. Tonight Calvert sees that he has shaved some lines into the side of his head. He thinks they look like the pathways of Alton Kellett, and perhaps that is what inspired them. He does not ask; does not care.

'Who says?' Calvert asks instead, taking the extra parsnip pyramid and levering it into his mouth.

'It was on the grapevine,' replies Redbone. 'And the news too.'

'What trouble?'

'Pig trouble, Ivan. They reckon the cops have put the word out that they're planning on spoiling the free festival.'

'Well, that doesn't surprise me,' says Calvert, whose rejection of all forms of authority matches that of his friend, though for entirely different reasons. His is born out of the experience of being on the other side of the barbed-wire authoritarian fence, while Redbone's has been shaped by too many free-party shakedowns and unnecessary free-festival confrontations.

'There's going to be convoys, sound systems, performances, all the usual shenanigans – the whole lot,' says Redbone. 'Enough cider to stun Somerset too. All the stuff that we've been doing over at Stonehenge on solstice day since the dawn of time, basically. Thousands of years that place has been a tribal route, you know. I remember a few years back, before they began to crack down, there were tents and caravans as far as the eye could see. There were dogs and kids running around, free food for anyone who wanted it. Bonfires. River swims. All the freaks in one place. Christ, one year I remember I copped off with this trust-fund crusty who spent half the year slumming it in the Crass house in Essex and the other sunning herself in the Med.'

Redbone whistles and shakes his head at the fond memory.

'I fell asleep in her van at midnight and woke up in Rouen.'

'Ruins?'

'*Rouen*. In France. I didn't even have a passport. And that wasn't even that unusual a weekend for me at the time. But now the fascist foot soldiers want to wade in with truncheons swinging. You know what they say.'

'What?'

'ACAB. All Coppers Are Bastards.'

Redbone has seen Europe. He has scurried across its face like a rat. He has seen its sewers – or at least the human equivalent: punk clubs on the underground touring circuit.

While Calvert was overseas serving in HM Forces, Redbone's rudimentary guitar-hitting abilities, and sniffer-dog-like knack for seeking out drugs wherever he found himself, endeared him, for a few years, to several bands whose membership was the gateway to many of the needle-strewn, phlegm-flecked squatted hot spots in Berlin, Paris, Amsterdam and much worse places. (Ferentari, a bombed-out-looking neighbourhood in Bucharest, Romania, for example, where a fellow band member awoke in a puddle on the concrete floor of the 'venue' the morning after a show with bleeding stumps where two fingers had been; he claimed no knowledge of the event and concluded they had been stolen by some young scamps with bolt cutters for the sheer hell of owning an Englishman's digits.)

The bands that Redbone played in while his friend was away training for – or fighting in – senseless wars all had one thing in common: empty noise was their only expression, and their appetites for indulgence far exceeded ambition or ability. They existed not to make music but to challenge reality, each band regressively more obnoxious and inept than the last, their legacy little more than some memorable nights for twenty, thirty or forty of Europe's most disaffected and dysfunctional young people and a trail of barely listenable seven-inch singles that littered squats and illegal clubs from Prague to Palermo, each discordant din of a release having sold just enough to keep the respective bands in petrol, Rizlas and falafels.

Yet still, having seen all that, and aware that there is plenty in his country's past to feel shameful about, and not being remotely patriotic, it is nevertheless England that fascinates Redbone the most. England pulls him in, and under. He feels its radicles reaching down deep into the bedrock of a place he loves as much as he hates and hates as much as he loves.

Even the rain.

Even the rain is a familiar vocabulary, a comfort of sorts to him.

It is a comfort because here is all he has known, ever since he was a hunched, hairy-backed primate roaming the wooded marshlands.

Perhaps it is because he knows he has always lived here, and that this is just the latest in ten thousand lives, and there will be ten thousand more if the great rotating mess of a planet manages to survive humankind's dire colonisation, which, in his darker moments, he keenly doubts it will.

'Plastic police,' sniffs Calvert. 'That's what I call them. Pigmy amateurs. They'd have not lasted five minutes at Goose Green.'

'It all came to a head at the Battle, anyway. We showed them then.'

The Battle was the Battle of the Beanfield in 1985, at which Redbone was a more than willing participant, and a subject that Calvert has frequently indulged his friend in over the intervening years but which he has little desire to hear repeated now, or indeed ever again, for the account is well worn and the telling of it is like retreading a desire path through the vegetation of Redbone's semi-fictionalised personal history. Calvert has long suspected that his friend somehow equates that June afternoon with some of the blood- and mud-flecked battles that he himself was a part of in South Georgia, when of course they are incomparable. He keeps quiet, though. Instead he lets Redbone relive his past glories once more, reasoning that all people are comprised entirely of their revisited formative experiences and elaborated stories, even if some choose to keep them buried in the catacombs of memory. In a voice lowered slightly for dramatic effect, Redbone continues.

'Yes, the sky was busy with bottles and bricks when they charged us, I tell you. We messed up a few of them good and proper, though. Oh yes. And it feels like yesterday. We should be there in case it all goes off again.'

'Not me.'

'We should be showing solidarity.'

'Not me,' says Calvert again. 'The sarsens of Stonehenge will be there long after the party has ended, and long after those plastic pygmies are bone dust in the damp dirt. None of this is anything new. They don't like people like us because we live freely, that's all. You know it and I know it. They see us doing exactly what we want with our lives and it fills them with fear because we've got the jump on them. I mean, philosophically we're way beyond them. We laugh at their stupid rules and their stupid little lives, their laws and their paperwork, their borders and their boundaries, and they can't handle it. The rich long ago decided they were going to carve up the country and God forbid any of the rest of us tread on their turf. It has always been the way but it just so happens that this current lot in charge are even worse than their predecessors.'

'Still.'

'Still nothing, Red. Leave them all to their little scraps and their pyrrhic victories. I'd rather be out here, making magic from that which is around us. If I've learned anything it's that beauty is more important than conflict. Beauty above all else. And you, my friend, have created a beautiful blueprint that will be less than useless if we stand here gassing any longer.'

Redbone thinks about this for a moment, and then decides he agrees with his friend, and solemnly nods.

They pack away their Tupperware and part again to wade out to their respective positions at opposite ends of the Solstice Pendulum, their simple tools held in clammy hands and slung over strong shoulders, treading further and deeper towards the centre of the landlocked sea.

Around them, the hills of England are sentient like mattresses stuffed with secrets.

Pylons watch on, hulking metallic skeletons that are joined wrist to wrist by cables that supply the hungry houses built too close together in the nearby estates. They thrum with sinister energy. Their spines straight and shoulders pushed back, the pylons remind Redbone and Calvert that they are trespassers and interlopers, yet in order to live as free men they must continue to do what it is they want to do, and that is to transgress the order that has been placed upon their fellow citizens.

They work at the furthest points of the field, away from the roads and tracks, the lanes and fences, the stiles and wires and borders and boundaries, deep down in a mapped-out place of covert creation, a temporary new cartography unfolding in their wake. Here is a place where time turns to sand and then blows away, irrelevant. In these moments, modernity itself crumbles and a form of time travel takes place.

And tonight, as during all the nights that have gone before and those that will surely follow, it is by taking this journey that in just a few sweaty hours two men are able to produce something that will baffle, beguile, provoke and amaze.

So they do.

They do.

O

'It's funny to think that the sea is out there.'

Having marked out the majority of the pattern, they meet in the middle of the Pendulum, and all that remains is to flatten the crop in the dominant circle. To do this one of the men usually drives a stick into the centre with a rope tied to it and the other end looped around his waist, and with a flattening plank underneath one foot embarks upon the long, lolloping circulatory walk of decreasing revolutions.

The sight of Redbone pulling the rope through the belt loops of faded black jeans that are held together by patches, safety pins and improvised stitchwork suddenly makes Calvert think of an emaciated donkey he once saw tied to a post on the fringes of a dusty Kenyan savannah that he passed through on his way from Nairobi to Tanzania during training manoeuvres. It feels like a lifetime ago, a hundred lifetimes ago, yet he remembers it as clear as a glass of water. He had assumed the donkey, captive and worked to the point of exhaustion, had merely been tethered to the post by its owner, but only now, only here and now in this moment, thousands of miles away in a field during the last dark hours of midsummer – the last of a decade that began with a short-lived sense of hope that he now dismisses as youthful naiveté and plain ignorance – does it occur to him that it might in fact have been laid out as live bait to lure the dangerous predators that had recently been raiding the local farms of their working stock. It was the look in the donkey's eyes that stayed with him; it was the look of one who is broken and now accepts whatever fate may await them, for all power or control has long been relinquished through force. It was not dissimilar to some of the Argentinian kids he faced across the sodden fells on those dire outcrops in the thrashing ocean.

Unsure as to whether Redbone heard him, or if he even spoke at all, Calvert says the words again.

'It's funny to think that the sea is out there.'

Redbone looks around him. 'Where?'

'Anywhere. Always.'

'Yeah, I suppose,' says Redbone, and then adds, 'It's easy to forget that we live on an island.'

'Not for me,' says Calvert. 'I see reminders everywhere. I've spent enough time on other islands to recognise that we have an islanders' mentality here.'

Redbone sets off walking, while Calvert follows to check the neatness of the circle's perimeter and gently stamp down any stray tufts so that the Trapping St Edmunds Solstice Pendulum will look like it could have been imprinted in the crop by who-knows-what. That is for others to speculate about, and reading the absurd theories in the papers and magazines, and eavesdropping on conversations concerning *their* covert work, is one of the best parts of their endeavour. The who-knows-what is part of the fun.

'Do you think?' says Redbone, over his shoulder.

'Definitely.'

'But what does that mean? How do you define an island mentality?'

'It means that, once, we looked to the horizon, and we wondered what lay beyond, and then set out for it. We colonised and plundered, and then when innocent people had been slaughtered and their resources accrued, we returned with riches. Then we turned inwards to slowly fester and moil in our own bitterness for a century or two, fearful that someone would one day do the same to us. Believe me, I know because I've been a part of it, but never again. Never again. The sea is a border, a boundary, and living on an island like this makes us think we're something special. But we're not. We're just scared, that's all. We're scared of the world. And that breeds arrogance and ignorance, and ignorance signals the death of decency.'

Redbone knows that his friend is referring to his many months spent down in the Falklands, a subject he never presses him on. Seven years have passed since his return and still Calvert can only broach the subject of his experience of the conflict, what he calls 'the make-believe war', obliquely and in his own time. Snatched references to night ops and the occasional passing mention of nick-named former comrades – Lofty, Crooksy, Chicken Livers – are all Redbone is privy to. But he knows that, behind the sunglasses and beneath the beard, even out here in the fields at night while focusing on a task, Ivan Robin Calvert is processing his past in order to survive the present. The future, however, is too perilous a prospect to consider and this suspected shared fear is another unifying factor in their relationship.

Over time Redbone has pieced together a ragged tapestry of these brief recollections and curtailed anecdotes; a fleeting memory here, a casually dropped bit of military slang there, or the occasional mention of a public-school-bred superior. The internal scars that Calvert carries are much more complex, an imbroglio of buried shame and anxiety, and far less visible than the tight twist of hot shrapnel-blasted flesh that marks his face.

Life for Calvert is a cracked egg. He is the shell and Redbone knows he is still trying to hold it together.

He also knows better than to press him further, for Ivan Robin Calvert is occasionally prone to breaking from his usual clipped and economical speech patterns and into these rare and unexpected soliloquies that give a momentary glimpse into the bottomless well of bitterness and trauma that runs deep into the core of his being, the orange yolk in his fragile egg.

Tonight, as they approach the gleaming pinnacle of summer, is not a time for dwelling on the past. Instead it offers a few fanciful stolen hours in which they intend to make their mark upon the canvas of agricultural England once more.

Necessity demands it.

O

Their operation complete, Redbone and Calvert pack away their planks and rope and begin the long walk back on weary legs. In their slightly frantic outrunning of the rising solstice sun, they have worked quickly – quicker than they would have liked – but it has still taken the best part of eight hours, with only a few minutes' break. A full night shift.

'I wonder how the boys and girls are getting on over at Stonehenge,' says Redbone.

'They'll be alright.'

'I feel like I'm missing out on history.'

'Missing out?' says Calvert. 'Missing out? You're making history, my friend. These crop circles are breaking new ground. No one has made works like these on such a great scale as we are doing. And that they've come from your mad mind should be a personal point of pride for you. We're way ahead of the game; right across Europe they're still trying to replicate patterns we ditched two summers back for being too simple. The things we are creating this year are going to resonate down the ages. Their power will grow. Trust me, we might not be famous but we'll be the first. And the best. Always. So don't talk to me about missing out on history.'

Redbone smiles at the affectionate admonishment. 'That's true.'

'You could be out there, dodging truncheons with the rest of your tie-dyed patchouli-drenched pals, but I think deep down you know you've already ditched those escapades for something more subtle. Something more subversive. Something *legendary*.'

'Fuel the myth,' says Redbone. 'And strive for beauty.'

'Exactly. And mess with their heads in other ways.'

'Well, if you put it like that, I'm all for messing with heads. Hey, look.'

Redbone stops walking and drops to a crouch. Calvert follows his sightline and does the same. They wait a moment and then raise their heads from the crop. In the next field they can see shapes moving about in the first mournful minutes of daylight as the unseen, waking, soft-focus sun reaches out to scour away the darkness. Sounds reach them then: bells and chants and a solitary drum emanating a pulse beat.

The final flames of a dying fire succumb to ash and embers as bodies sing and sway around it. They are all women. They are all naked.

'I see your mother and her pals are having another Women's Institute meeting,' Redbone says with a sanguine smile, and quick as a flash Calvert smacks him playfully – but hard – around the back of the head.

'Cheeky bugger.'

They watch for another minute or two before Calvert says, 'Bloody pagans. Come on, you, we're not perverts. Let's shake a leg.'

The summer solstice weekend saw an unprecedented amount of disruptive activity across Wiltshire, Somerset and Hampshire. Arrests were made near Stonehenge when a 'peace convoy' crashed through a police roadblock during an attempt to visit the sacred site, which is closed to the public. Several hundred hippies and 'New Age travellers' drove across fields and cut down fences in the lead-up to a violent confrontation. This disturbance mirrors the 'Battle of the Beanfield' in the same location in 1985, which saw the windscreens of police vehicles and buses smashed and unlit petrol bombs hurled when riot police intercepted the Stonehenge Free Festival. It was the largest mass arrest of citizens since World War II.

'We just want to be able to commune with the stones in harmony,' said a traveller spokeswoman and mother of two, Arianna Peace Frog. 'It's a time-honoured English ritualistic tradition to congregate at the 'Henge and celebrate the sunrise together – men, women, children and all God's creatures – on the longest, brightest day of the year. We're peaceful people, but the establishment see the way we dress, our haircuts and the amount of freedom that we have and consider it a threat to the order of things, so they've come down hard. They envy us. I was at the Battle of '85, and this was just as ugly.'

Seventeen arrests were made, and a number of travellers hospitalised.

Several illegal 'acid house raves' also took place in remote rural locations across the region, attracting thousands of revellers, many of them high on drugs such as cannabis, ecstasy and LSD.

Elsewhere further 'crop circles' have appeared across the south-west region, most notably at Trapping St Edmunds, where a design dubbed the 'Solstice Pendulum' has attracted many visitors, including academics and experts in paranormal activity, who arrived en masse to examine the intricate circles and corridors of its two-hundred-and-fifty-foot-long design.

Gazette & Herald,
24 June 1989

LONGBARROW WHALE
(ABANDONED)

Again, Redbone asks: 'Did you see it?'

'Yes,' replies Calvert, without the need for further explanation this time. Because he knows. He did indeed see it.

They are parked on a roadside verge near an undulating grass-covered slope that, though marked by the concentric lines that denote rising landscape, is not significant enough to actually be given a name on Calvert's worn OS map, though it is known locally and colloquially as Black Milk Hill. He looked it up in the library's local history section and discovered that the name dates to the mid-1700s, when a herd of cattle grazing on this natural earthwork was the first to be suddenly stricken with a panzootic of the highly infectious and ultimately fatal virus known as rinderpest. As it was reported, the herdsman recalled seeing his cows expelling black milk shortly before they expired: 'Black droplets did fall from their dugs and they was all unsteady on their legs and, oh Lord, I did consider perhaps the world it was a-ending.'

The hill cowers a half-mile or so outside of the village of Gypsum Great Bassett and a few hundred yards past the last old cottage in the hamlet of Short Longbarrow, famous for a cache of Neolithic artefacts including flint arrowheads, a sickle blade, shards of pottery, hide scrapers and six ceremonial cups that were unearthed here in 1822 during an excavation led by the controversial archaeologist and antiquarian Prof. Forbes Fawcett-Black of Oxford University, and for being the birthplace of a former *Blue Peter* presenter.

Over the other side of Black Milk Hill, the land levels out and wheat fields stretch for miles. In a few moments they will circumnavigate its lower slopes, cross one field and then begin work on the Longbarrow Whale, so-called because of the elongated oval-shaped design. Though not Redbone's most sophisticated work, it bears a similarity in silhouetted profile and size to that of a whale. It is also a reference to two of their pioneering works from last summer, Pine Farm Turtle and Haxby Dolphin Triplets, and therefore serves as a quiet clue for those closely following the evolution of crop circles – a suggestion of continuity in creation. The latter design in particular left scientific investigators perplexed and conspiracy theorists energised and excited when they discovered that the three dolphins that created a bird's-eye triptych in the crop were positioned so as to form the three sides of a gigantic isosceles triangle, with one length shorter than the others, the vertex angle measuring a mathematically perfect 36 degrees and the two base angles similarly measuring a perfect 72 degrees. Such dimensions form what is known as a golden triangle.

It was a feat of mastery so precisely executed, and on such a huge scale, that a year on it is still drawing widespread bafflement and many conflicting expositions. So-called scholars came from as far away as Mexico and Japan to examine the clockwise weft of the crop and study such disparate subjects as local ley lines, lunar cycles, protean microclimates and previous UFO sightings across the county in order to expound their array of colourful and often hysterical theories, all of which Redbone and Calvert found laughably way off the simple truth of the matter. The work was also covered by several major national media outlets, including the BBC *Six O'Clock News*, whose rather dry piece aired the night after activists had interrupted the live broadcast to protest against the new Section 28 law, which limited rights for homosexuals, and which inspired one tabloid newspaper headline that very morning: 'Beeb Man Sits On Lesbian'. As a result the Haxby Dolphin Triplets inadvertently achieved record viewing figures, with viewers tuning in the next night to see if anything quite as exciting might be repeated. At that point it was, undoubtedly, their finest hour. But that was a year ago and the pair's ambitions are now far loftier.

'It was something, wasn't it?' says Redbone, referring to the coverage afforded to the Trapping St Edmunds Solstice Pendulum.

'A cracker.'

'I think we nailed it, Ivan.'

'That we did, Redbone.'

'I mean, it didn't reach the *Six O'Clock News* this time, but we're back in the big-word broadsheets. We even got a spread in the *Telegraph* alongside the battle with the pigs at the 'Henge.'

'I didn't have you down as a *Telegraph* reader.'

Redbone shrugs.

'I like to keep abreast of things, view the prism from all angles, you know? Also it was one for the scrapbook.'

Calvert smiles to himself. He doesn't do it often, and Redbone thinks it strange to see his friend's rare expression, like seeing a dog smile, but is also aware that something used sparingly has power too. It is only the smallest of smiles, a half-smirk that momentarily escapes the framework of his otherwise passive expression and is then suppressed almost as quickly as it appears, yet it nevertheless has greater value as a result. Seeing Calvert approaching something approximating happiness makes Redbone happy too.

'Shame the paper didn't name it,' Redbone continues. 'Maybe "Trapping St Edmunds Solstice Pendulum" was too much of a mouthful.'

'You're forgetting that only we know the real names,' says Calvert, 'though they sometimes come close. Some of them seem to get through.'

'Oh yeah.'

He pauses, and now Calvert can hear the greasy engine of his friend's mind ticking over.

'I feel like, with each new pattern that we pull off, we're edging closer to the big one. The biggest of all. The one we've always talked of, dreamed of.'

'The . . .' says Calvert.

In his excitement Redbone cannot contain his enthusiasm. The words tumble out, an involuntary interruption. 'Yes, yes. The Honeycomb Double Helix.'

Calvert shakes his head with reverence at the very mention. In a low voice, Redbone continues.

'Picture it: dozens – no, scores – of circles in ascending diameter running in three curved tendrils that trail centrifugally to create a fractal that resembles something seen in deep space or under a microscope, or maybe never seen before, as this beauty is coming from the deep, deep subconscious. All my daydreaming, all my doodles, all my trips, journeys and life experiences will be going into this in ways that even I cannot comprehend. We're talking next level. The motherlode. I've already been working on some initial plans.'

'You'll have to show me.'

'Ah, but most of it is up here,' says Redbone, tapping his scalp with one yellow-tipped finger.

'Good lad. A sound security measure, that. You're learning and thinking like a soldier.'

'I'm learning from the best.'

Again Calvert smiles but this time they both feel awkward at the shared moment of overt comradery, and quickly erase the signals.

'It's a team effort and a team is only as strong as its weakest member,' says Calvert. 'Fortunately for us, we have a tight little cell and the correct division of labour: I scope out and recce potential sites and lead the nocturnal sorties, while you, my friend, come up with the more – what's the word for it again? – that's it, the more *esoteric* side of things.'

'Well, anyway,' says Redbone. 'We're not ready for the HDH. Not yet, no way. The design I have has only revealed itself in parts so far, a close-up detail at a time, because even I am not ready to receive the full pictogram. I reckon it'll be a two-night job at the least, and one that will require a very special field in a very specific location. I'm talking a kilometre long here, and we're still out of practice.'

'You're right there, soldier. But nothing that can't be created in a night is worth doing. Returning to the same place is a no-no. It's in the code, remember. But I'm already scouting for the correct canvas. I envisage a perfect patch framed by other fields, accessible, yes, but far enough away from civilisation so that people have to make an effort to get there, and with a nice hill nearby to provide a natural viewing station. I've earmarked Tuesday and Thursday next week to embark on a couple of one-man recon sorties.'

'Good, because although we're not ready,' says Redbone, 'I don't think England is ready either. And that's half the fun. Because when we drop a Honeycomb Double Helix on the nation, tiny minds will be blown most regally.'

'Correct. It's more or less our duty. Especially after reading some of the stories in the papers. There's plenty of the usual UFO rubbish, but this time they're quoting academics on the matter, which makes it even funnier – as if having letters after your name suddenly gives you licence to talk even more sweet bollocks. Silly sods. People just want to believe in something bigger than all this. Something beyond. It takes them away from the mundane details of their tiny lives. You can't blame them.'

O

The night steals their thoughts for a few minutes. It drags each man off in a different direction, their feet trapped in the stirrups of a galloping beast called rumination.

'We're going to have to get going in a minute,' says Calvert finally, in a voice as flat as Norfolk. 'A van with two men in it is dodgier than an empty one round these parts at this time of night. We're too conspicuous sitting here like show ponies.'

Redbone ignores him and pursues the unstoppable thoughts that are racing across the terrain of his mind.

'Do you ever think about why we keep returning to the fields, though?'

'I think I've just answered that. Because it takes us away from the mundane details of our tiny lives too.'

'But I mean, do you think there are reasons why we keep returning to the fields specifically, rather than, say, nicking scrap metal or growing leeks or playing golf or whatever else it is that normal fellas like you and me do.'

Calvert groans like a squeezebox. 'Well, firstly, there's a strong argument against us being normal fellas. And secondly, you have permission to take me out with a clean headshot if you ever see me playing golf. I'm serious, hire a sniper, it'd be a mercy killing. I could give you a couple of numbers to call. I wouldn't see it coming, but I'd surely deserve it.'

Redbone laughs and then, when he has stopped, he starts up again.

'But, yes,' Calvert continues, 'I know why I come out here to the fields week after week, summer after summer. Anyway, come on, we should get going. We have a whale to bring to life.'

'I feel like it's an instinctive thing for me.'

Impatient, Calvert sighs. 'Well, me too.'

He reaches for the handle, opens the door and steps out into the warm stillness of Wiltshire. Sombre Black Milk Hill looms over him. In the Stygian silence the dormant mass appears to have grown in size. It seems wakened now too, as if in possession of a beating heart, or that at any moment it might stretch and rise to its full height, shake off molehill soil, wind-blown branches and 1970s picnic litter just as a wet dog shakes river water from its coat, and then stride purposefully off across the landscape. A shiver of excitement runs up Calvert's back at the sight of it; the endless potential of the night is an excellent fillip for the deep inertia he has been experiencing.

He feels like a poacher, part-creature, at one with all around him: a snapped twig underfoot, the fluttering leaves. The whispered admonishments of the wind in the trees.

'The need to just be out here, creating greatness in silence, is strong,' says Redbone in a low voice beside him. Even in his sunglasses, his headtorch dazzles Calvert, who, when he blinks and closes his eyes for a moment, sees the glare of its bulb repeated in the dark void of momentary blindness.

'Yeah,' he mumbles. 'It's addictive.'

'But now and again it pops into my head at the oddest of times – when I'm jamming with the band, maybe, or washing up – what my true motivations are.'

'You? Washing up?'

'What?'

'I just can't picture it. Anyway, I know what motivates you, Redbone.'

'Do you?'

'Of course. Trespass and confusion. Myth-making. You've said as much a hundred times yourself.'

'I always just assumed you weren't listening.'

'Torches off,' says Calvert.

'What?'

'Off,' he hisses. 'There's a car coming.'

He huddles by the far-side wheel arch of Redbone's old van and gestures for his friend to join him. A moment later a police car rounds the bend and comes towards them. It slows as it passes the van and they feel the beam of the headlights wash over their feet like chalky floodwaters as they lean in tight, making themselves small.

But it does not stop. It passes by.

'Christ,' says Calvert.

'It's OK,' says Redbone, standing. 'They've gone. It was nothing.'

'What if they clocked your reg plates? What if they run a check?'

'It's fine.'

'Now they'll be able to trace the Longbarrow Whale to us.'

'It's all covered. It's fine. The paperwork is done.'

Redbone bends and carefully removes the registration plate from the front of the van. Beneath it is another, very different one.

'If they run a check they'll find that this fine vehicle is all registered and paid for.'

'Really?' says Calvert, genuinely surprised that Redbone has bowed to convention.

'Yes. By one Sir Cyril Wallace.'

'Who's he?'

'Esteemed former Tory MP, and once keenly vocal exponent of field sports, particularly the callous pursuit of our vulpine friends – that is to say, fox hunting. And now currently deceased, or certainly at least for the foreseeable.'

'Excellent work. But why would someone called Sir Cedric Wallace drive such a hunk of junk? It's just not credible.'

'Cyril,' says Redbone. 'And I don't know. But if we get the van moved now we won't have to worry about that eventuality.'

O

The Longbarrow Whale does not require a great deal of coordination, but it does require a huge amount of simple crop trampling. Redbone and Calvert split off in different directions, but first they ensure that there is consistency in the way the wheat is flattened. They have seen too many circles and pictograms created by amateurs where the crop has been left a chaotic mess, which they agree not only looks aesthetically lazy and gives craftsmen such as themselves a bad reputation, but is also potentially fatally damaging to the harvest, and therefore likely to incur the ire of both the tenant agriculturalists and their wealthy landowners. And invoking such anger and opposition will surely, in turn, increase the policing of their patches, when they already have growing interest from the various theorists, journalists and assorted nut-jobs to contend with.

'The key here,' Calvert remarks, 'is to draw *just enough* attention.'

Redbone is working in the wide-open space that constitutes the main trunk of the whale when there is a rustling noise in the crop and a hare comes tearing out of the wheat. It runs straight towards him along an old tractor wheel path that intersects the Longbarrow Whale somewhere near its centre, and where no crops grow.

Startled, the hare spots him at the last minute, and he sees its eyes held open wide with fear, its nostrils flared and probing as they seek scents in the motionless moment, the sinewy muscles of its long limbs flexing. Before the hare stands a thin man wearing raggedy clothes, a jacket tied around his waist and mud-caked boots whose leather is as cracked and lined as the face of a ragged man excavated from a primordial bog. His hair is pulled up into unkempt punkish tufts, held there by various types of matter unknown, and there is a rope held between his hands and looped through a plank underfoot. The figure could be a scarecrow, were it not for its hot human smell and the fact that it goes by the name of Redbone. For one trusting moment man and hare are locked in unspoken communication, a wordless transaction as old as the pastures and meadows themselves, as timeless and sure as the dry July soil beneath their tired feet. But then the hare makes a sudden tight right turn and veers back into the crop with an acceleration that is more impressive than a score of stupid roaring cars endlessly circling a track to the delight of thousands, many of them sporting baseball caps. Redbone savours the solitude of this interaction, this display. But just seconds later there follows another hare, as fearful and harried as the first, and then two more in rapid succession.

There is more rustling across the body of the pictogram and then Calvert appears, scuttling like a strange bent beast of the barley.

'Hares,' says Redbone, pointing. 'Loads of them.'

Another makes a break across the island of flattened crop. He points.

'Look.'

Then for the second time tonight both Redbone and Calvert see a beam fan out before them, but this time it is a single ray of light, and though its origin is a hundred metres away at the bottom of the next field, it is still much more powerful than those of the earlier police car. Juddering unevenly, the light moves through the field and towards the corner where they know there can't possibly be a track.

'Look,' says Redbone. 'It's like a will-o'-the-wisp.'

The crack of a gunshot splits the night somewhere over to their left. It is insultingly sudden, obtrusive. It's almost physical, the way in which it appears to put a hole through the centre of everything.

'Lampers at three o' clock,' whispers Calvert. 'These twats will shoot anything whose eyes are caught in their beam. They don't care what. Look at that mounted lamp – it's massive. I bet you any money that's an open-topped jeep they're driving. Ex-military. I'd recognise that engine growl anywhere.'

From where they are the vehicle sounds like a mosquito getting closer.

'You mean they're some of your old lot?'

Calvert vehemently shakes his head. 'Hell, no. No one from the regiment would pursue helpless creatures for fun at night, messing up good farmland like that. No way. Cold-hearted is what this crew is.'

This makes Redbone angry and his voice curdles with reciprocal violence. 'I'd like to see the tables turned. I'd like to see *them* thrown out into the fields without their weapons and given a ten-count. It's them that should be hunted.'

Calvert snaps a wheat stalk and chews at the soft fleshy part of its base. He squints towards the light, says nothing. They hear the engine getting louder. Closer.

The beam from the mounted lamp bounces erratically across the crop. A few grounded pheasants clumsily take flight. A lean frightened fox runs across the incomplete Longbarrow Whale at speed, like a flaming arrow.

Calvert spits out part of the gnawed stalk.

'We're going to have to abort.'

Redbone turns to him and looks at him with eyes pleading towards the half-dark. 'But we're nowhere near done.'

'Abort and retreat.'

'We've never aborted before,' says Redbone, his voice strained with rising frustration. 'Never. *Never*.'

'Well, we're going to have to now. They're headed this way.'

'There's a fence between us.'

'Doesn't matter. Look at them: they'll plough through anything. Gates, fences, crops, they don't care. And for what? All to bag a fox, a badger, a few hares. Even pet cats sometimes. And they call it sport. A bullet would be wasted on this crew.'

'I blame Black Milk Hill,' says Redbone. 'I'm sure that thing is alive. I could have sworn it moved before when my back was turned. But then when I looked at it, it had moved back to where it originally was. It has put a curse on the night.'

Calvert does not dare admit it, for to do so would suggest irrational thought and that in itself would signal weakness, but he has felt something similar too, a foreboding presence like a breath at his collar, a sense of unease blossoming like a black flower from a deeply rooted seed of instinct. It is the same sense of instinct that brought him back depleted but alive from that dismal archipelago down on the Patagonian Shelf to a vulgar hero's welcome that was as stage-managed as a West End musical.

They watch the jeep careering about the next field as more shots are fired and more sleeping birds take flight in a fearful fulmination.

'Look at them,' says Redbone with disgust. 'They're not true countrymen. Me, I'd like to dig a bear pit to catch them. A nice deep, dark bear pit in the middle of the field, big enough to drive a jeep into. With pointed stakes. Now there's a sport I could get involved with.'

'It's just our bad timing that this tanked-up bunch of clodhoppers have chosen this field, that's all,' says Calvert as he strokes his dense beard with his open palm. 'Although you have given me an idea. I'm going to need you to take these and head back to the five-bar gate we came in over.'

He hands Redbone his rope, planks and camouflage-coloured knapsack and then takes his headtorch from his pocket and straps it on.

'Wait for me there and then we'll leg it to the motor the back way, through that deep patch of bracken that we came in through.'

'Why, what are you going to do?'

'You'll see. Meet me at the five-bar.'

Still stooped, Calvert scurries across the flattened patch of whale trunk towards the next field, where the jeep appears to have paused, its lamp trained away from them, but instead of standing he drops down onto his belly and monkey-crawls under the fence and into the crop. Redbone sees the stalks wobbling for a few yards as Calvert carves a trail through, and then all goes still and silent. Readying himself for retreat, Redbone lifts the coil of rope over his head and one shoulder, and wedges the thin planks beneath an arm. He can feel his heart full of hot blood, the blood pulsing in his temples. Temples drumming a blast beat. There's a flush of adrenaline working its voodoo magic too. Mouth dry, skin prickling.

A minute passes before there are three gunshots, and then a voice rings out, clear and vehement in delivery. It bellows at full volume.

'*WANK TROGS.*'

Calvert appears from the crop and stands at full height. His voice is clear and his headtorch is flashing intermittently like the light that accompanies a siren.

'*NEEDLE-DICKED WANK TROGS,*' he bellows again, louder still.

The mounted lamp on the jeep spins around but it is too slow, for Calvert has already dropped back out of sight and is, Redbone guesses, stealthily monkey-crawling through the wheat stalks towards the intruders again with speed and agility. The jeep rides roughshod over to where his friend first appeared.

Sure enough his head pops up, but he is way over to one side now and Redbone thinks of the fairground game he played as a child where you had to bash toy lemmings with a mallet. Calvert shouts again and this time he jumps up and down, waving his arms, headtorch still flashing. Mad bastard, smiles Redbone. My pal the mad bastard. But he is only there for perhaps two or three seconds, just enough to be seen, to make himself a target, before disappearing back into the golden profusion of wheat once more. Redbone watches on intently, as if it were all a scripted film projected onto the screen of night.

The jeep changes its route and now Redbone can hear voices as the beam from the mounted lamp bounces and the vehicle charges indiscriminately through a crop that is only a few weeks away from harvest – a crop worth thousands of pounds, but worthless if crushed and ruined.

Calvert appears close to the lampers now, dangerously close, and the jeep only has to adjust its course slightly as it accelerates towards him.

But then he is gone before they see him.

The jeep charges in his direction for two, three, four seconds and then there is a grinding noise and the sound of shouting as the bright white beam tips forward and comes to an abrupt standstill, lurching at an odd angle. The jeep's horn sounds – loud, abrasive and unstoppable. It is a wanton wail in the statue-stillness of the trespassed night.

The lampers have hit a drainage ditch and Calvert has lured them into it.

Redbone cannot contain his joy. He leaps to full height and punches the air, shouting in triumph, then swiftly turns on his heels, his worn mummified boots gripping the dry dirt, and runs directly across the middle of the Longbarrow Whale like a mammal breaking cover, through the thick crop that surrounds it, and then turns left onto a tractor path that leads him back to the five-bar gate. Calvert is already there, barely out of breath, his dark shades brightly reflecting Redbone's own bobbing white torch beam.

'How did you get back here so – '

Calvert says nothing. Instead he vaults the gate with a flourish.

'That was *amazing*,' says a breathless Redbone as he struggles to keep up. 'That was a night's work worth abandoning just to see those cretins crash nose-first into the ditch.'

'Come on, let's get out of here.'

'Needle-dicked wank trogs, though?'

'Not my best line,' says Calvert as he reaches over the gate to take the rope and planks from his friend. 'But, you know, I was improvising.'

O

Black Milk Hill is less of a sinister presence as the sun rises above the crooked horizon line of the farmed plains beyond it. It is a dawn without fanfare, a sullen daybreak that creaks with a sense of reluctance. While Redbone is still revelling in their victory over the lampers, and chattering excitedly about his friend's display of cunning, Calvert can't help but feel tender and scratched up inside, as if he were a pane of glass that might crack and shatter at any moment.

He is not out here at night to get dragged into conflicts; quite the opposite, in fact: he is here to escape such everyday ills of humanity that continually threaten the carapace he has grown around himself.

As they climb the hill, Redbone detects the change in mood and he too stops talking. Despite their minor victory, his friend's unspoken anger is implicit. Soon they are at the crest of this cursed landmark, where the medieval murrain was said to have struck all the beasts that grazed here.

They turn and sit, and there below them is the Longbarrow Whale, abandoned. Past it, close to the perimeter fence, they can see the back end of the jeep jutting out from its drainage ditch – a ditch more than likely dug in several centuries ago, by men like Redbone and Calvert, and perhaps by men like the lampers too. Behind it, a trail of destruction winds through the crop. Its destroyers have fled the scene.

Viewed from this vantage point, the partially realised pictogram leaves a sour sense of bitterness that burns and stings their stomachs. Having to leave a piece incomplete in this way slowly corrodes their morale, though their fertile imaginations can at least fill in the gaps so that the scale of what it might have been still remains impressive.

'It's like the *Venus de Milo*,' says Redbone. 'Incomplete.'

'The *Venus* had arms once.'

'Oh yeah,' says Redbone.

'As did hundreds of other such similar marble Greek and Roman sculptures, no doubt. It's strange, isn't it, to think that history is littered with snapped limbs and stolen hands.'

'Well, anyway,' says Redbone, 'we'll do better next time. We'll make sure of it. I've something up my sleeve.'

Calvert nods. 'Surely. And I've scoped out somewhere a bit special.'

'Where?'

'Just by Bracklebury.'

'I don't know it.'

'You wouldn't,' says Calvert. 'It's very obscure. Very remote. But soon enough everyone will know the name of . . .' He pauses. 'What's this new design of yours?'

'It's something inspired by snails.'

'Snails?'

'Apparently they were held in high esteem in ancient Britain. Their shells have been found buried beneath excavated megaliths, so they must have had some importance. They used to call them dodmen and their gluey trails were called ladders, while their shells are works of mathematical wonder, if you look into it. So I thought I would pay homage with circles and swirls and giant antennae on stalks. We're going big. What's the site called again?'

'Bracklebury.'

'Then we shall return in style,' says Redbone, 'with the Bracklebury Dodman.'

More strange occurrences this month in the south-west counties, where crop circle chasers claim to have disturbed a pattern, mid-creation, in what may be the closest encounter yet. For the past three years Swindon couple Clive and Joan Winters have dedicated many of their summer nights to driving the back lanes of Wiltshire, Somerset and Hampshire in the hope of discovering and documenting definitive evidence of this strange phenomenon.

'We always try to retain an open mind,' gas-fitter Clive told the *FT*. 'These patterns could be willingly created by unknown visiting beings in order to communicate coded messages or they could be the accidental by-product of their landing crafts, we're just not certain.'

'It has certainly made a pair of night owls of us,' adds wife Joan, a local authority clerical assistant. 'Our neighbours probably think we're strange, disappearing every night and returning with the milkman, but to us it's both research and a hobby. Some people collect stamps, we document crop circles.'

During a recent excursion, the couple claim to have interrupted 'several small beings' who had embedded themselves in a field's crop beside Black Milk Hill near the village of Gypsum Great Bassett.

'There were lights flashing intermittently at strange angles, like silent sirens – one moment in front of us, and then the next far away,' says Clive. 'We also heard what sounded like voices, but they were speaking a language that was completely indecipherable, and in a register that was both higher and lower than the human range. I'd describe them as the grunts and bellows of insidious creatures. When we examined their markings, there was a near perfect whale-like shape and a strange smell in the air, but they also destroyed a jeep in the field, possibly as a warning to not come too close. It had been lifted and dropped like a toy car. We took a series of photos but when we had them developed the film was corrupted, which leads us to believe that these entities do not want to be seen. We shall keep returning until they do.'

'It's costing us a bomb in petrol,' added wife Joan.

Fortean Times, July 1989

BRACKLEBURY DODMAN

Purple lightning strikes a pitchfork fracture with violent precision in the evening sky. Abrupt, jagged. With it goes the last of the light, as if a dimmer switch has been impatiently turned, and somewhere far away a dog barks and the futile sound of a car alarm goes ignored by all who hear it.

Then comes the thunder, growling like a cornered dog, rumbling like a two-day hunger.

Rain rattles the roof of Redbone's van, each drop urgent.

It builds into a sustained military tattoo, and for two or three minutes the storm is a sustained attack of pure summer violence so vast and indiscriminate it appears it may never end. But it does, finally slowing to a meek and easy splatter, and pregnant drop-lets hang like tiny silver baubles from the branches caught in the white glare of the headlight beams.

They are parked down a dead-end lane, Redbone and Calvert. To one side, behind a spiteful tangle of witchlike hawthorns, is an old pond once used as a watering hole for animals, and where, years later, local children would come to swim and frolic, but now it is fenced off to the world, and no children swim or frolic here. Their anxious-eyed parents, city-born transplants into the grow-ing suburbs, have filled them with a trepidation for their natural surroundings and pumped them plump with horror stories. The parents prefer to keep them within sight now. Fresh fears have replaced traditional ones, and a different sense of policing takes place now, though it is all grounded in an intolerance for the unknown.

So the pond is a dark and dire neglected place obscured from view, and only noticed this night when a skein of geese comes crashing down upon it, alarming the two men as they sit in silence. The moment passes, the geese settle and the rain continues its mesmerist's act with metronomic precision. Scowling, Calvert sniffs the air around him.

'It smells like cheap market-stall beef in here. Are you living in the van again?'

Redbone nods glumly.

'What's up?'

'Xanthe has kicked me out.'

'Xanthe?'

'Yes. She booted me out the flat and changed the locks the next morning. That is what you call a non-negotiable development.'

'Sorry to hear that.'

Redbone shrugs as Calvert frowns and turns to look at him.

'Wait a minute – who is Xanthe? I thought you were going out with Astrid.'

'I was. I am. That's partly why Xanthe kicked me out.'

The rain continues to hit the roof like a drab Sunday's parlour clock, tick-tock.

'But you were living with Xanthe?'

'A bit of both, really.'

'A bit of both?'

'Well, yes. These were situations dependent upon certain ever-changing factors.'

'Such as?'

'Oh, all sorts,' says Redbone vaguely. 'It was actually a very mature and progressive set-up – for a while, at least.'

'And Xanthe gave you the elbow because she found out about Astrid?'

'Well, she knew about Astrid all along, but that was solely a weekday thing, whereas I always saw Xanthe at weekends. It worked out OK for everyone. But then I started staying out all night and sleeping all day so she barely saw me at all, except when I was snoring with barley grains in my hair.'

'From doing the crop circles?'

'Yes, exactly that. I mean, I couldn't exactly tell her what I'd really been up to at the weekend, could I, so I had to keep coming up with excuses as to why I was turning up for breakfast on Sunday knackered and stinking, and then sleeping right through until teatime. She thought I was having an affair.'

'But you were. With Astrid, I mean.'

Redbone shakes his head emphatically. 'Oh no, no. An affair is when it's undertaken in secret, when it's an illicit thing conducted on the sly. I've told no lies, apart from my far-fetched alibis about what it is we get up to, you and me. No, you see, Xanthe thought I was having an affair with someone else. Everything was fine through last autumn and winter because I was about all the time, or at least at the weekends, anyway, but then spring came round and our circling season began again, and I was gone. I was dust. I was out here with you instead, fuelling the myth, striving for beauty. And Xanthe said she reckoned I must have been shagging a scarecrow, the state I was coming back in, covered in straw and mud and tick bites, like a stray dog. That's what she called me: a stray dog. Can you believe that?'

'Hey, there's nothing wrong with dogs,' says Calvert. 'They're not daft. I've not met a single dog who has a job or has to pay taxes. Will she change her mind?'

'No. The toothpaste's out the tube now. There's no putting it back in again.'

Occasionally Calvert wonders what it might be like to have a woman in his life, or not even a woman but *someone*, for his approach to sex and his own sexuality has always been one of mild confusion and frustrated indifference. He knows he is meant to feel certain things such as desire or need, yet he resolutely does not, never has, and suspects he never will. Beyond this realisation, he has never felt compelled to pursue the question mark of his sexuality any further than his own mind.

From a young age he has regarded his genitalia as a visitor, a sort of innocuous intruder who places no demands upon him but is just simply there, a functional entity rather than a weapon to be waved about. There have been experiences, of course there have, but they were limited, embarrassing and unsatisfactory, and therefore rarely bore repeating. Pornographic magazines passed on to him, their spines cracked and pages occasionally glued together, were briefly thumbed and then discarded like last year's catalogues. They held no interest. In certain situations in the Forces, particularly in those first few months of training, he occasionally found his eye lingering longer than intended in the showers at the various, grossly differing, appendages of his fellow soldiers, as if they somehow held the answers to the question of what he was. But the questions remained unanswered and his eyes averted, and he long ago began to define himself only by that which he is not: a rampant stud. He is a man, yes, unequivocally, but not one of these braggadocious beasts you see down The Feathers or The Lion, or any number of pubs, clubs or places where men gather to boast about their latest conquests, even if so many of them are fictional.

Perhaps the beard and tattoos and sunglasses have gradually become one way of deflecting any such questions that others might ask of him, though he has largely ceased worrying about it, and all formative anxieties about his inability to be aroused or physically connect with others have more or less abated. And if Redbone has ever wondered about his friend in this way, he has never verbalised it. It is another reason why their friendship remains sound.

'So,' says Calvert, 'what does Astrid say about all this?'

'You'd have to ask Diamond Dale Hubert.'

'Who's Diamond Dale Hubert?'

'The bloke that's sleeping in my bed.'

Calvert looks at his friend with growing exasperation. Tonight his scar is a smooth silver disc of flesh, as if something hot was once pressed to the side of his face. A brand or an iron. Behind him, hissing rain splatters the passenger window.

'Diamond Dale Hubert is a DJ on the rave circuit,' Redbone elaborates. 'A pretty bloody good one, actually, I'm surprised you've not heard of him. He's top ranking on most of the flyers. But he only works weekends. He plays the illegal parties, acid house ones that last for two or three days, and then he's done, after which he's free all week, which is great for Astrid because when she gets in from selling her smiley face hoodies and bootleg rave tapes at the indoor markets and occasional car boot, he's there, cooking three-bean stews and rolling her joints. *And*, unlike me, he always has a wedge of cash to contribute towards the rent. Then, come the weekend, they both get their bellbottoms and bandanas on, rub themselves in Vicks, and have it big-time in the fields from Friday night to Sunday lunchtime, at which point they crash-land back into a day-to-day reality which, I think we all can agree, is, at best, banal. In many ways it's a marriage of convenience and I'd say it has worked out pretty well for them both. Good luck to them.'

'But not for you?'

'Depends how you look at it, really. Now I have total freedom, and you can't put a price on that.'

Calvert furrows his brow and takes a deep breath.

'To recap, then,' he says. 'Your weekday girlfriend Astrid has replaced you with a DJ called Diamond Dale Hubert and your weekend girlfriend Xanthe, who already knew about Astrid, now thinks you're having an affair with a third person, possibly a scarecrow, and has thrown you out, effectively making you homeless, so now you're living in this van that smells like a butcher's slop bucket.'

'That's about the sturdy length of it.'

Calvert pauses, befuddled, a question forming in the frosted windows of his hidden eyes.

'But – hang on a minute – did Astrid know you were seeing Xanthe on the weekends?'

'Of course. Xanthe is her sister. She encouraged it. It got me out of the way for a bit, and who can blame her? I annoy myself, and I'm me. My only real error is that I got everything upside down and the wrong way round, but the real irony of it all is, I spend more time with you than any of them. I just can't tell them the real reason why.'

Calvert takes all this in as the two men sit side by side in silence. Finally Redbone speaks. His voice is quiet.

'It's all still worth it, though.'

○

Ten minutes pass with little but the changing rhythms of the rain and their own gnashing minds to distract them. The thunder and lightning has blundered on to the next county over and leaves in its wake a lighter rain that seems to fall with more frivolity in the glare of Redbone's torch beam when he unfolds himself and steps out to urinate. He does so loudly and with no small amount of satisfaction. Like a bloody racehorse, he thinks to himself.

The rain reminds Calvert of drums because he has had the dream again. It formed in his midweek sleep, silent and fore-boding, like a longboat gliding through the mist. It is always the same dream. A huge dream, a dense dream. It fills every corner of his sleep like wet concrete, then hardens into the day there. In it he is a rebel chieftain of a small clan, a warrior stooped in the doorway of a low stone dwelling. Soft peat smoke billows from a chimney and he is wearing clothes made from the tanned hides of animals. Violence lurks just beyond the horizon; he can smell it. Sense it. The violence spreads like a fungus in the minds of men like him, men from other clans, where generations of blood feuds and vendettas with other clans have grown into a hatred and fear so solid and monolithic and towering that it blocks the sun, and so threatening to their entire existence that it must be smashed to shards because there are women and children to protect. Only he, Calvert, stands between them, between the women and the children and the shrieking menace just beyond the horizon. He hears drums. He is scared.

The drums get louder.

This is the dream. This is how it ends each day upon waking, huddled on his mattress beneath itchy military blankets in his little loft space.

'So what do we do now?' asks Redbone as he climbs back into the van with his hands on his zip, and with relief Calvert returns to the modern moment.

'Do?'

'Yes.'

'With regards to what?'

'We'll get soaked.'

'The rain has nearly stopped.'

'I mean out in the fields. We'll get soaked through.'

'Does it matter?' says Calvert.

Redbone is smoking a roll-up using only his lips to manoeuvre it. As he exhales smoke through a small gap at the side of his mouth and an even smaller gap in the window, he pictures his friend huddled in a foxhole freshly dug into stiff soil with a folding spade. He sees him soaked and shivering, his sodden clothes leaden and clinging to his white body, his cold and nervous fingers curled around cold black metal. He remembers what he's read about the Battle of Goose Green, and the scant details that Calvert has shared with him, one tiny grim morsel at a time, and he remembers the hostile pieces of land jutting from tempestuous waters that were fought over for little more than political gains back home. He tries to imagine how it must have felt knowing that death stalked those lonely knuckles of rock in the subantarctic, so far away from everything that his quiet and thoughtful friend knew. He thinks of the frigates and the light cruisers and the guided-missile destroyers suddenly struck without warning, or sunk at sea during air attacks, on both sides, the heavy grey waters swirling in and over the last funnel of light as the seabed beckoned, the taste of salt consuming the screams of men. And he thinks of the men maimed, around two thousand in all. He thinks of the men killed. Nine hundred or so. Women too, including three native civilians shot down in friendly fire. Friendly fire, Redbone thinks, as if such a thing could be possible; as if a gun could ever be considered benevolent.

He exhales more smoke, nips the stub of his roll-up between his fingers and puts the crooked end in an old tobacco tin on which there is a picture of a big-eyed Martian.

'I suppose not.'

'So tonight we shall incorporate the ultimate ring, then, true and round,' says Calvert. 'The perfect golden circle.'

Redbone twists his face.

'Actually, there's no such thing. Or at least not one that can be created.'

'How do you mean?'

'The perfect circle. We could never make one. They don't exist. In fact, I don't believe anything man-made can ever be perfect. If you attempted to draw one – by which I mean drawing one circumference line that is precisely evenly distanced from its centre – even with the world's keenest eye and steadiest hand the ink from your pen would let you down as it would not be evenly distributed.'

'Pencil, then?'

'Graphite is just as bad, probably even worse. But you're missing the point, which is: there's always a flaw somewhere; that's what makes us humans rather than machines.'

'Ah,' says Calvert, 'but who makes the machines?'

'Humans.'

'Well, then.'

'Well, then nothing. Show me a machine that is perfect forever. No, machines break down; none of them last. And the same rules apply to their attempts too.'

'Computers, then? I bet a computer could draw a perfect circle.'

'No, because eventually the image will pixelate.'

'What does that mean?' asks Calvert.

'It means even the thinnest of lines eventually becomes a series of polygons and therefore the circle becomes corrupted or distorted. If you ask me – and it sounds like you are – the closest to the perfect circle is in nature, and even then it only appears that way. The moon in the sky, a newborn baby's opening eye. And of course they are spheres rather than circles, which is something else entirely. And anyway, they too are far from perfect. Believe me, I've looked into this stuff *a lot*. Engineers have tried and failed because if you zoom in close enough, no circle or sphere is evenly balanced on a micro-level. We could go in even deeper, even closer, to a subatomic level, but still no circle or sphere is absolute. They're always a bit . . . off. Basically, perfect circles can't be created, certainly not by two blokes in a field with some rope and grand schemes and visions. Sorry, my friend. The perfect circle can only ever exist as an idea. Which, when you think about it, is no bad thing because that means we each of us carry one within us.'

'So, in a way, the perfect golden circle does exist after all.'

'Yes. In our imaginations only.'

'Where they are beyond corruption,' says Calvert.

'Yes,' says Redbone. 'I suppose that's true.'

'So they exist, then.'

'Not literally.'

'But they exist in our minds.'

Redbone sighs. 'As much as anything that does not exist can do so in the most fertile of imaginations, yes.'

'Good,' nods Calvert. 'I knew they did.'

O

The rain is a light patter now, as fine as iron filings, as weightless as sparks. Silence sits between them, during which a thought occurs to Redbone. It falls from his mouth before he has time to filter it.

'Do you still think about it?' he asks.

Calvert turns to look at him. At night his sunglasses seem absurd. At night his whole appearance seems absurd, though of course Redbone would never say so.

'Think about what?'

Redbone sniffs. He loosens some snot in his throat, winds down the window and then spits it out.

'Sorry, a touch of hay fever. About when you were away. When you were down there.'

He points a thumb downwards, and Calvert knows he means the underside of the world. He does not reply at first. He does not say anything for a long time, but Redbone knows that if he waits long enough an answer will come.

'At least once a minute of every waking moment of every day,' he finally says.

Redbone waits again, then he speaks. 'What is it like – war, I mean?'

They both sit watching the tiny drops of rain hit the windscreen.

'You've never asked me that before,' says Calvert. 'All these years, you've never asked me about it, and I appreciate that.'

He goes quiet again and there is just the gentle dancing rain, and the night. Redbone knows that Calvert is carefully choosing both his words and the correct order in which they must be arranged. His friend is masterful in his economy of language, poetic in his minimalist deployment of words. Nothing he says is ever without some point or purpose.

'War is organised confusion,' he finally says. 'At best it is that. And at its worst it is beleaguered kids shivering on a rock in a spiteful ocean, with nothing but cigarettes and antique weaponry with which to fight against elitist and indulged trained killers, all for little but the folly of others far away. War is a disgrace and all military organisations should be dismantled tomorrow.'

This is more than his friend has ever said on the subject so Redbone does not push it any further, and, really, what else is there to say anyway?

So again they sit saying nothing. Again there is only the rain and the dead-end lane, and the hawthorns and the black pond, and the things they have seen and done, the minor victories they have achieved and the great mistakes they have made.

O

Bracklebury Dodman comes easy. Apart from getting soaked all the way up to their chests from the sopping crop, tonight they do not have to labour at it. Even though the barley stalks are sagging beneath the weight of the water that each seed head holds, there is a freedom to the men's movements and an unspoken communication of what it is that they each must do in order to complete this creation. And after the thunder and the storm, the air has cleared. It has a fresh new scent, an earthen musk, and the July night is a folk song sung between the soil and the sky.

They are ahead of schedule when they stop for water and a snack.

'What have we got tonight, then?' asks Redbone.

'I've been a bit busy this week.'

'OK.'

Calvert looks sheepish.

'I have a new recipe for a spinach, chickpea and lentil pie – '

'That sounds delicious.'

' – but it wouldn't fit in the oven.'

'OK.'

'And I had other things on my mind.'

'OK. So?'

'So I call this *Malus Domestica* Surprise.'

Calvert reaches into his knapsack.

'*Malus* what?'

'*Domestica*.'

'What does that mean?' asks Redbone.

'*Malus domestica*. It's Latin for apples.'

'You brought apples.'

'Yes,' says Calvert, glad that the embarrassment in his eyes is hidden by his sunglasses.

'Right. And what's the surprise?'

Calvert pulls out two apples.

'The surprise is that I've only brought apples.'

He passes one to Redbone then keeps one for himself, sniffs it, buffs it on his thigh and takes a large bite, and then pushes his slipped sunglasses back up onto the bridge of his nose as he crunches noisily.

○

Finessing the final section of crop that constitutes the tip of the Dodman's final antenna, they fall into stride.

'I forgot to ask you,' says Calvert. 'Did you see that farmer?'

'Which one?'

'The one on the local news.'

'No.'

'The one at Trapping St Edmunds. You didn't see him?'

'No. I don't have a telly, do I? What about him?'

'He's put a padlock on his gate, set up a makeshift tollbooth in a chemical toilet and has been charging folk to see our Solstice Pendulum ever since he first set eyes on it. He's using raffle tickets.'

Redbone stops and laughs at this. He laughs loud and long.

'How much?'

'Fifty pence a head. He's coining it in, especially from all the dingbats. Apparently he had a research team of biophysicists from Bristol University, a coachload of Swedes. Plus there's the media, who have to pay double. There was even two fellas who flew in from Wyoming with some weird contraption they've built out of bike parts and aerials to prove that it was all clearly the work of alien visitors. They've been there every day for weeks now and have got more colleagues flying in to join them. Oh yes. It was all over the news.'

'Does the farmer give repeat visitors a discount?'

'Not likely. He's doubled down and is charging them to camp in the next field too. Free milk and butter, though, to be fair.'

Redbone laughs again, even louder and longer than before. For once Calvert does not tell him to keep quiet. They know that there is unlikely to be anyone around for half a mile or more in any direction. Not tonight. Tonight they might be cloud-drenched and dripping, but in this moment they are free from all thoughts of intrusion or interruption, past or future. They are in the present moment, living every second of the act of creation.

Not long after 4 a.m. they finish and trudge back to the van as the night drains away like dirty water, leaving them feeling as exposed as one who sits in an emptied bathtub.

'Look,' says Calvert, wincing slightly, 'we're soaked. You can stay at mine if you want.'

Redbone is taken aback by the offer. And though he appreciates the significance of the gesture, he also knows that he cannot accept it, for to do so would be to change the dynamic of an effective working relationship, and a friendship too, one based on discretion, space and mutual understanding. A friendship based on things largely left unseen and unsaid. He also knows that Calvert will almost certainly not make the offer again.

'I'm alright, thanks.'

'It's somewhere to get dry.'

'It's fine, Ivan,' says Redbone. 'There's a hot day forecast for the morrow. The sun will sort these clothes out. I thought I might go for a swim anyway.'

'A swim? Where?'

'I'm not sure. I quite fancied having a break from the dusty crops and the hum of the pylons and getting a bit of sea air in my lungs.'

Calvert grimaces at this. 'The sea's miles away.'

'The sea's never miles away in England. Besides, I've got a full tank and nowhere I need to be.'

'Please yourself,' says Calvert.

'Always do.'

O

The morning sun draws a mouse from the raggy bowl of grass in which it sits on its litter of seven tiny hairless mice, the black specks of their eyes still blind behind a film of pink skin. Its tiny nose cautiously sniffs the air before it slips down to the rain-softened ground, which in places is lightly steaming. High above it a buzzard circles, searching the soil for signs of movement, for rising moles. It does not see any but it does see that something has changed within its hunting grounds. The field is no longer solely a slow-swaying forest of crops. Now it bears the markings of man, of intrusion, for a vast and confusing pattern is imprinted upon it.

Wind lifts the feathers on its wing as it glides another wide circle, sizing up the landscape. The mouse does not see the buzzard. The mouse does not see a shadow-shape crossing the sun as it scurries out from the long crop and into one of the newly opened spaces. Now the buzzard spies the mouse, and it hovers here for a moment, suspended in the cool nowness of the sky.

An invisible line connects them like the taut string between a child and its kite. Then something gives, like gravity ceding to flight.

An enterprising farmer has been supplementing his income by capitalising on the sudden rise in crop circles appearing in fields across England. Peter Tempest-Stephens has been charging the hordes of visitors attracted to a work created during the summer solstice on his land at Trapping St Edmunds.

'If they're daft enough to travel all this way and go marauding across my crop, then I'm going to make sure I get something out of it,' said Tempest-Stephens. 'We've had professors, foreign tourists, all sorts of weird buggers. Hundreds of them. I don't mind whoever is creating these things being in my fields because they never make a fuss and they don't damage my wheat, but this lot are a pest worse than wireworms in my sugar beets, so I feel no shame in charging them. That's simple free market economics, is that.'

Financial Times,
14 July 1989

HIGH BASSETT
BUTTER BARREL
WHIRLPOOL

High Bassett Butter Barrel is a raised outcrop of land on which it is believed a fortress once stood, and is so-called because of its cylindrical shape. It looks like something pushed up from the bowels of the earth, or at least appears man-made, and is completely incongruous in the landscape of broad loping agricultural fields, ancient upland pastures and wide skies that at night hold the stars like argent-bellied herring in a faraway net.

That this steep-sided mound is natural merely increases its air of intrigue. Adds electricity to proceedings. Trees grow upon its flat crown and local mythology suggests that wood from this ancient copse was used to build the gallows in nearby High Bassett, upon which several women were executed in the seventeenth century following accusations of witchcraft. Naturally it is now considered haunted by a ghost called The White Lady, as so many small woodlands in England are.

The prospect of a tormented apparition seeking revenge upon mankind does not remotely bother Redbone when Calvert tells him. It doesn't bother him at all, for he believes that ghosts and hauntings are just the lazy way of acknowledging the transference of living human energy throughout the ages, and in fact is certain that he himself has experienced the pages of time curl back like a phone book tossed onto a fire. Indeed, on more than one occasion he has discovered that, if he stares at it long enough, part of the sky appears to peel back like a small sticker stuck on the skin of an orange, or the way the dimpled skin itself might succumb to the edge of a thumbnail dug in to reveal the pith and flesh beneath it.

But there is nothing quite so tangible beyond the sky, only the suggestion of infinite space that scares him a little, and thrills him even more, and makes his teeth itch at the dizzying vastness of the universe and indeed the possibility of an infinite number of universes beyond this one, if indeed infinity could even be numbered.

Then, when he has pulled his eyes away from the sky, it has felt like pulling the rubber suckers of childhood arrows from the cold glass of a window of a house he struggles to remember.

Redbone knows he has felt past eras breathe through him. He has seen time's fabric tear, and through the gap he has glimpsed his past lives many times over. In flashbulb moments as brief as the flicker of a strobe, he has seen yellowed boar tusks – his tusks – rearing up as he charges through the undergrowth with ravenous dogs barking at his broad back. He has watched standing stones being hefted into place on barren plains. He has seen bonfires and blood. Soil and smoke. Naked wild women and men with missing limbs. Heard the sharp and stringent wind whistling between the gaps in a hill fort of stones.

He knows that he carries the past and the future within him, and for Redbone it is not a burden, for he has walked the old earthworks at night, seen the steam rising from the sleeping stock's nostrils. He has watched the eagle drop and kill. Stood by a great poisoned lake entirely devoid of life. Seen future cathedrals collapse and common species become extinct. Tower blocks crumble. Watched the tide wash over church spires. The seas rise and rise. The crop wither.

All lives past and present sit within him.

Of this Redbone is certain.

So the prospect of a ghost that stalks a wood for all of eternity is not something that unnerves him, not least because by tomorrow morning High Bassett Butter Barrel will be known for a new addition to its surrounding landscape.

Calvert's thoughts on the fluidity of human life are somewhat more problematic as, with almost clockwork regularity that he now recognises as being intrinsically tied to the changing seasons, he often wakes to find himself enveloped by a crashing wave of despondency that, at its worst, threatens to be near fatal. This usually first occurs in mid-September, when the summer finally releases its grip on the land and retreats backwards into impending darkness. Where Redbone sees life as a thrilling continuum, Calvert considers it a conundrum that can never be solved, only endured.

In these moments he feels like driving to the coast and then walking out into the sea until the weight of the water lifts him up and carries him off into the great salty broth of the Bristol Channel, or perhaps leaving his boots behind on the sandbanks of Hampshire and just disappearing into the swirling currents where the Solent bleeds into the English Channel, gone forever, a festering fleshy food for the crabs that crawl across the ocean floor.

Fortunately he does not pursue this possibility as he does not own a car, and the sea is over fifty miles away, and public transport in England is, at best, erratic and unreliable, and would almost certainly require a convoluted journey which, in his darker moments, Calvert simply cannot be bothered to plan or undertake. When these moods fall upon him like a dozen hefty wardrobes, just getting out of bed and semi-vertical in his crawl space becomes near impossible. Instead he lies there and remembers a comedy scene – he can never recall the film or TV show – where a character says he would drown himself but he cannot swim, and then Calvert smiles at the absurdity of it all, and reminds himself that the road of life is full of potholes and that the best that anyone can hope for is that the smooth planes in between are frequent and prolonged.

'Tomorrow we're going to make what I will call a whirlpool,' Redbone explained as they once again bent themselves conspiratorially over drinks in The Feathers – cold cider for him, ginger ale and *not* ginger beer for Calvert, a point he remains emphatic about. 'But not just any whirlpool, I want us to craft one so big and strong and mighty that it looks like it could suck the sky down into the guts of it all. Something so awesome it's scary. And so scary it is awesome. It'll act as the perfect counterpoint to the thrusting spectacle of High Bassett Butter Barrel.'

'I'm in,' Calvert replied without hesitation, his teeth aching with the sugar hit from his cold drink and a small, almost coquettish, belch escaping him. 'Let's shake them right up. Let's make their fillings rattle, their tits tinkle and their balls clack like castanets.'

'As far as I know the whirlpool has never been done before. Or not one like this.'

Redbone then discreetly showed him his many etchings for an elaborate design of circles within circles, but where each was positioned in an off-centre way so that the entire pattern appeared to be vacillating or boring down into the core of the planet itself.

'Wow,' said Calvert, which was the greatest expression of wonder that his friend had ever heard him utter. 'You're way ahead of everyone.'

He picked up his half of ginger ale, which looked lost in his meaty hammer of a hand. Redbone just smiled back.

'You know they're going to be trying to replicate this one for years to come,' Calvert added. 'And they will fail – because the first is always the best, and everything that follows will just feel like an unoriginal replica, a hollow homage. A simulacrum. Crowds might flock to these future versions, and people might be impressed, but those in the know will be able to say, with a great deal of certainty, that whatever they produce – and by whatever means – it will never be as good as the High Bassett Butter Barrel Whirlpool. Because, with your permission, that is what I think we should call it.'

As Calvert enthused, Redbone silently noted to himself just how animated and exuberant his friend had become over the past week or two. He had rarely seen him like this before, and certainly never in the sunless months of autumn and winter when he tended to fester in Bluebell Cottage, or sit brooding in The Feathers of an evening, his feet planted to the floor, sunglasses in place, facial scarring turned to the shadowed corner of the back bar as he sullenly sipped his ginger ale and sought respite for a few hours from the chorus of raised voices inside his head, while he went through the motions of pretending to be a normal, fully functioning member of society, which of course Redbone knows he is not.

Calvert was still talking.

'This is *the* crop circle, the archetype. The ultimate.'

'I'm glad you think so,' said Redbone. 'But I do already have plans beyond it. Plans for bigger and better things.'

'I'm sure you do,' said Calvert. 'I'm sure you do. But there's something about this thing that's both strange and familiar at the same time. It's close to cliché, but avoids becoming so. Christ, man, this one looks alive. It almost looks like it is oscillating. It's . . .'

Calvert leaned forward and looked very serious as he searched for a word just beyond his reach. Then he grasped it and behind his shades his eyes widened.

'It's *visionary.*'

Redbone beamed back, basking in the glow of Calvert's unexpectedly effusive compliments. They clinked glasses and raised a toast for tomorrow.

O

July has crawled to a close. At Calvert's suggestion they have decided not to work on a Saturday night this time, just in case the crop spotters happen to be out. After their long night in The Feathers, as Redbone retired to his van, Calvert took the latest designs with him and shoved them into his wood-burning stove, which had been inactive since spring, save for these ceremonial eradication rituals featuring Redbone's increasingly labyrinthine drawings.

The summer has become busy with the crop spotters as they descend upon the fields like locusts. Wave after wave of them have been arriving, a small plague of people sporting tan shorts and bumbags. Some bring transistor radios and deckchairs and make a long weekend of it, parking their cars on the roadsides at angles that block passing tractors. Several farmers have reported finding human faeces on their land. One even discovered an abandoned kayak in his cornfield.

Wherever Calvert and Redbone go, the crop spotters follow, often only a matter of hours or even minutes after they have packed up and driven off down dawn lanes to enjoy a hearty Full English at the nearest service station. And not far behind these first crop spotters, who seem to materialise as swiftly as maggots follow death, come the news crews: cameramen, sound operators brandishing boom mics, and stiff-backed reporters pronouncing well-used platitudes into microphones. Sometimes there are helicopters overhead, often more than one at a time as they compete to get the first shot of a virgin design. A good photograph of a crop circle that has never been seen before can now be sold for thousands of pounds to the broadsheets and the tabloids, whose hunger for this new phenomenon is only growing more insatiable with each new work. Urgency is everything, and also the circles fill up valuable page space at a time when newsrooms are depleted of staff due to the summer holidays. A striking photo and a simple one-sentence caption can fill half a page, or if an amazing design coincides with a particularly quiet news day it might even occupy the front cover. This is the jackpot for all concerned, except the circles' creators, who remain largely indifferent to everything except the act of creation itself.

Without realising it, Redbone and Calvert have become two of the highest-grossing new visual artists in the country, though of course they do not receive a penny for their work, nor would they wish to. Neither is it strictly their art that is for sale, but miniature reproductions of it in newsprint – or, as Calvert calls it, 'Tomorrow's chip-shop wrappers.'

So they have taken a night off from fieldwork and broken their own disciplined work schedules in order to throw the crop spotters and newshounds off their trail, before meeting on this late Sunday evening to head out to the furthest location from their village yet. It takes well over an hour to get there.

As Redbone drives he has one hand on the wheel and the other dangling out of the window, trailing the air with his wiggling fingers. At this speed the air takes on a sense of liquidity, as if molten matter is all around him.

Only now does he realise that they are passing close to the old wetlands; in fact they are only a mile or two away. The wetlands are home to many breeding birds and a popular stopping place for several migratory species, and he considers his role in preventing a bypass from being built over this precious green space several years ago as perhaps his greatest achievement in life. Now, whenever a formation of geese flies overhead, he likes to imagine that they are honking their gratitude specifically to him. Redbone recalls the protests, the banners and the linked-arm picket lines as a war general might a particularly successful campaign. It instils in him a sense of pride and purpose, with the non-existent bypass just one more enemy crushed underfoot and buried in a non-existent unmarked grave while the last post is sounded on a bugle of the imagination. A wonderful time. Such victories, he believes, are what define a person.

Calvert turns round in his seat. He eyes a mass of electrical equipment in the back of the van. There are amps and speakers and strange black boxes. There are guitar cases and pedals, neon-coloured drumsticks and a snare drum whose skin is split.

'What's all this?'

'Band stuff.'

'I thought you weren't playing any more?'

'It's for a new thing I'm putting together. Top-secret project.'

'Oh yeah? What style is it this time?'

'Grindcore shit, but with a strong acid house influence.'

Calvert frowns. He looks confused. Shakes his head. But says nothing. His face is a zipped tent.

'I'm going to new extremes,' says Redbone. 'We'll have a live drummer *and* a drum machine. Maybe two. A triple attack.'

'You're not doing rural West Country reggae any more, then?'

'I'm not sure I ever was? Besides, no one else is doing anything like this.'

'For good reason.'

'I'm working on a bass frequency that will make people cack their kecks.'

'A growing market, I'm sure,' says Calvert.

'It's the sound of the future, my friend.'

'Then God help us all.'

O

It's a domineering and incongruous presence in an otherwise flat plateau of prime agricultural land, High Bassett Butter Barrel, and every now and then both Redbone and Calvert pause in their labours to look up to its tree-covered peak, where a chorus of owls echoes between the sturdy timber trunks of its much-mythologised copse. The owls are so owlish that they resemble a sound effect, a dusty vinyl recording found in the BBC's audio archives. The tree trunks meanwhile create corridors and the owls echo down those corridors as if a needle is stuck on the record that is playing continually in an empty office deep in an abandoned building guarded by a solitary nightwatchman for whom retirement cannot come quickly enough.

No one ever calls the noises they make 'owl song' because they are entirely devoid of melody, but instead are weighted with expression, warning calls made by small feathered sirens.

Redbone and Calvert walk in circles from the outside in, and the motion feels like a form of beautiful madness.

They walk for hours, for miles, each lost in the task, their thoughts, the meditative still nothingness of their slowly emptying minds.

'Sebastian.'

There is suddenly a voice behind them. A female voice. They both jump. Then there it is again, louder, closer.

'*Sebastian.*'

They don't even have time to hide as a moment later a figure comes shuffling through the towering wheat stems and out into the central clearing.

A torch beam flashes first at Calvert then at Redbone, and in the glare their faces become crumpled white rags of confusion before Calvert turns on his headtorch in response. A very small, very elderly woman stands before them. Redbone thinks she may be the shortest, oldest women he has ever seen. Her head is small and her skin is very wrinkled – like a baked potato, he thinks. Or a jar of pickled walnuts found in an overgrown gazebo on a country estate.

She does not appear afraid at the sight of the men before her.

'Oh, what are you doing out here?' she asks, but before either of them can reply she answers herself: 'You're farmers, I expect.'

'Yes,' says Calvert, cutting off Redbone, who he knows will more than likely say something too close to the truth.

'You don't look like farmers.'

Her voice is high and stretched; tremulous. Redbone imagines her handwriting to be similar, like a daddy long-legs dragging its excitable body across the page.

'What do farmers look like?' he says.

The woman thinks about this.

'Red cheeks, a bit shifty. Odd-looking, you know. And with string holding up their trousers instead of belts.'

'We're organic farmers,' says Calvert. 'We have belts.'

'You what?'

'We have belts.' He enunciates this slowly and clearly.

'No, the other bit.'

'Oh,' says Calvert, already regretting the lie. 'I said we're organic farmers.'

'What's that?'

'It means all the produce comes from the soil.'

'But doesn't all – '

Smiling, Redbone interrupts the lady. 'It just means no pesticides,' he says in a soft voice. 'All natural. Anyway, it's us that should be asking you what you're doing out here alone, in the middle of nowhere at this time of night. This is private land you're on, you know.'

He doesn't mention that they do not own the private land and that they too are trespassing. He has doubled down on the gamble that this isn't *her* land.

'Well, it might be the middle of nowhere to you boys, but not to me. I know this place like the back of my hand. Better, in fact. And I've not seen either of you before. I never forget a face, though I wish I could forget a few.'

'We tend to work nights,' says Redbone. He nods to Calvert. 'He has a condition that makes him sensitive to direct sunlight.'

'Yes, I wondered what that mark on your face was,' replies the woman. 'I imagine the sunglasses are to do with that too. Anyway, I'm looking for my Sebastian, have you seen him about the place?'

'I don't believe we have,' says Redbone. 'What does he look like?'

'He's quite swarthy, with long hair in good need of a trim. Broad shoulders, strong features, no knackers.'

'No – ?'

Calvert interrupts Redbone again, and in a gentle voice asks, 'Who is Sebastian?'

'Well, he's my dog.'

Redbone smiles at this, but then out of a delicate sense of diplomacy that the situation demands – and sympathy that the old dear evinces in him – swallows it as if it were an oversized aspirin.

'Has he run off?'

'Obviously, yes. Yes, he has.'

'Near here?'

'Yes, in this very field.'

'Well, we've both been out here working for a while and I'm afraid we've not seen him,' says Calvert. 'Was it tonight?'

'No.'

'Earlier today?'

'No.'

'Yesterday?'

The small old lady shakes her little walnut head. 'No.'

'When, then?'

'July the twenty-seventh,' she replies. '1909.'

Calvert flashes a sideways glance at a baffled Redbone, who looks as if he is about to say something but then hesitates mid-thought, his features rearranged into a question mark. He really is terrible, thinks Calvert, at disguising what he is thinking.

'1909,' says Redbone. 'As in, eighty years ago?'

He turns to his friend then and Calvert raises an eyebrow in response. The eyebrow speaks volumes, and those volumes feature only two words: *Humour her.*

'Oh, I don't know,' says the woman, counting on crooked fingers. 'Let me think – yes, I was a young girl of thirteen, so it must have been something like that. You see, we were out walking one morning – a nice day, it was, just like this one – and he put up a hare, a bloody big hare, and before I knew what was happening he tore after it like the clappers, but Sebastian must have got lost out here in the fields because I spent hours calling his name and looking for him, but he never came back. Maybe he kept running or maybe the hare took him because they say the devil lives in hares, and if you ever had the chance to look in the eyes of one close up, you'd surely see him in their eyes there. But one rarely does because they can run like the devil too; they'll be four fields over by the time you get your boots on. That night my father and older brother came and they looked too, but still there was no sign. Perhaps little Basti could hear us calling for him, but couldn't find his way back to us. Or maybe the hares had him, and were teaching him to do a merry dance in the moonlight for their own amusement. Or perhaps they put the gloves on him and made him do a few rounds. Either way, I'd have thought he must be getting hungry by now. That's why I bought this, just in case.'

She takes from her pocket a tin of chopped pork.

A thought suddenly occurs to Calvert. 'It's July the twenty-seventh today.'

The old woman's face brightens. 'Is it really?'

'Yes.'

'Well, fancy that.'

'He must be getting on a bit now.'

'We all are, dear. We all are.'

Redbone asks, 'And do you come out looking for Sebastian often?'

'Oh yes. Quite often. When my new hip permits.'

'Always at night?'

'I don't remember. I have a torch, though.'

'And do you come out here alone?'

'My brother used to help me.'

'Right.'

'But then he got killed.'

'I'm sorry to hear that,' says Redbone, and he is.

'It was Ypres,' she says in a curt, matter-of-fact manner. 'It was the war. The great one. You probably heard about it. Terrible business. All the mud. So now I look alone.'

She begins to call the dog's name again. 'Sebastian. *Sebastian.*'

Redbone glances at Calvert once more, who imperceptibly shakes his head at his friend, as if to say: *Don't.*

'We – '

Calvert shakes his head again.

'We could help you look,' says Redbone. Calvert's face sinks but Redbone merely responds with a shrug.

'Oh, would you? I wouldn't want to disturb your farming, but that would be very kind.'

'It's no problem. It's no problem at all. We both love dogs, don't we, Ivan?'

Calvert's rictus grimace is so ridiculous it makes Redbone want to roar with laughter.

The three of them fan out in different directions and call the dog's name. Calvert notices that Redbone is calling with a real sense of conviction in his voice, and in a way that strikes him as completely absurd. In fact, it is one of the most ridiculous things he has ever heard. But still, after only a few minutes he too finds himself calling out 'Sebastian, Sebastian', with an undertone of hope to the words, and for a few brief moments he even imagines that the dog might yet come bouncing through the high summer's glistening bounty, his long uncurled pink tongue lolling, panting as he greets them all with great excitement and several stories to tell of his time with the drove of hares.

The little old woman meanwhile appears oblivious to the fact that she is criss-crossing the gigantic half-finished crop circle of High Bassett Butter Barrel Whirlpool.

After ten minutes she comes over to Calvert.

'Well,' she says, 'it looks like little Basti is staying out for one more night.'

Redbone pushes through the crop to rejoin them.

'I've checked down the bottom end, right to the fence,' he says. 'There's plenty of rabbits, but no Sebastian, I'm afraid.'

'I'm sorry we couldn't find him,' adds Calvert.

'That's alright. He's a tough little bugger and the weather is good. I imagine he'll show his face soon.'

'He might even be back home waiting for you,' says Redbone.

'Now there's a thought.'

'And if he's not,' says Calvert, 'then there's always tomorrow.'

'There is indeed,' she nods. 'There is indeed. Well now, you men better get on with your farming. What is it that you're growing out here?'

'Well,' says Redbone, at first unsure as to whether she is joking or not, but when he sees that her question is as earnest as her quest to find her dog he replies: 'Wheat.'

'Ah, wonderful,' she enthuses, looking around her as if seeing the crop for the first time. 'No cows?'

'No cows.'

'No pigs?'

'No pigs either.'

'I don't suppose you'd have sheep round here either.'

'No,' says Redbone. 'No sheep. Only arable.'

'Well,' she says brightly, 'goodnight, then.'

'Goodnight,' the two men reply in unison as she turns and departs, disappearing deep into the crop, into the arcane mystery of the humming night once more.

O

'Shame about that dog,' says Redbone wistfully. 'I wonder if he'll show up.'

Calvert looks at him. He looks at him until it feels like the crops have withered, the seas have risen and the sun has burned itself out to an ashen cinder.

He shakes his head.

'I do wonder about you sometimes.'

O

Before they leave, they convene in the very middle of High Bassett Butter Barrel Whirlpool's main circle. Calvert crouches down and, with a deftness of hand that suggests he has practised this many times over, carefully plaits the strands of the crop where they meet in the epicentre of the Whirlpool into a woven knot as neat as a harvest loaf. At its heart is a small hole just inches across.

'A circle within a circle within a circle,' he says, standing. 'Now it's finished. Now it's golden.'

He reaches into his rucksack and pulls out a packet of his hard dry biscuits.

He puts one into the hole.

'For Sebastian,' he says. 'Just in case.'

Now it is Redbone who stares at him. He stares until the sun is reignited and the unsullied morning of a brass-coloured Monday beckons.

'Song for the Circle'

Time's coarse tongue calls it
High Bassett Butter Barrel
but the gods do not deign
to name it so.

All they know
is that the circle of life
spins, Gaia suckling
all on her golden aureole.

And the silent hill watches over.
Haemorrhaging history.
Bleeding out beautifully.

The Poet Laureate, July 1989.
Written on the occasion
of the growing prevalence of
crop circles in England.

CUCKOO SPITTLE
THOUGHT BUBBLE

The night is balmy but the sunken lane is as dark as ink. Hedgerows hem the two men in on either side and without torches they would be unable to see either their feet or their hands in front of their faces. Wiggled fingers become disconnected, abstract, digits only to be felt or guessed at. For a few moments they try walking without lights and darkness absolute enfolds them.

Though they try to stride with purpose, the two men's steps are tentative so as to avoid pitfalls and the plethora of tiny perilous chips of gravel that, when jarred underfoot, can send a man slipping arse about tit as if he were on a sheet of winter black ice.

Moths like ash ride the night's light draught in the bright white beams of their headtorches, which, viewed in tandem from a distance, give the impression of a tall vehicle bobbing down the constricted lane.

Redbone and Calvert let their other senses guide them. Taste, touch, sound. Smell, even. They smell a way through. Because the threat of danger has a scent too: that of dry dust and electricity, like an old television cooling in the corner of a living room where something indescribably bad has just happened.

A form crosses their path at speed. Caught in the white glare of their beams, it is a low-scuttling misshapen creature – hunched, alien and diabolical. It is a small thing but with a massively oversized head, and the proportions of its body all wrong. Only when it pauses for a moment to look their way do they see what it is: a weasel weighted with the sagging corpse of a freshly killed rabbit clamped in its jaws, a rich reward for the merciless questing hunter in the short night's pursuit. Its eyes are viciously indifferent to them.

The hedgerows too are violently alive with activity as all around Redbone and Calvert the life cycles of creatures are played out like a tightly choreographed ballet whose only great certainty when the final curtain falls is death for some and survival for others.

It hasn't rained since the stormy downpour that fell on the night of the Bracklebury Dodman. Not a single drop has dampened the county and everything feels brittle to the touch. The leaves on the trees have become leathery and clumps of old moss have turned to powder, as delicate as puffballs.

The land is parched and on some agricultural plots huge sprinkler systems have been deployed to keep certain crops hydrated. Miles away in the uplands the reservoir levels are dropping, and there has been talk on the news of introducing a ban on hosepipes, families having to share their bathwater with one another. The region is a day or two away from being officially accorded drought status.

The field to which they are walking is the most steeply sloping that they have visited. It has been scouted by Calvert exclusively to host Redbone's latest work, a curving crescent of conjoined circles increasing in size up the hill so as to give the appearance – though it is not meant to be one – of a caterpillar whose large 'head' contains within it in the elliptical shape of a crescent moon. The scale is so vast as to be silly: over four hundred feet from end to end.

'I can't decide whether to call it the Caterpillar or the Thought Bubble,' Redbone pondered upon revealing it on a picnic table tucked away in the far end of the beer garden out the back of The Feathers. 'Or The Scorpion. Or – *no, wait* – maybe The Dragonfly Larva? That doesn't really slip off the tongue, though, does it, and I suppose it depends on what works best with the name of the location. It has to sound like it is at least approaching the poetic, otherwise why bother. Ugly names are no more palatable than ugly faces or ugly places, am I right?'

'Cuckoo Spittle,' replied Calvert. 'That is where we're headed this weekend. It's a series of fields marked on the Ordnance Survey map as Cuckoo Spittle Meadows. It's near no village but it's still a risky job. A good spot, perfect for this design. This pictogram.'

'Risky how?'

'Well, the land abuts a large country estate and you never know who is lurking about those places. It belongs to the Duke of Something-Something and we all know what these aristocrats are like.'

'Do we? I can't say I've met many myself. They're not big on the crust-punk scene.'

'Well, half of them are nuts, aren't they?' said Calvert.

'It's all the interbreeding, I expect. Cousins boffing cousins will send a bloodline squiffy.'

'I know some of the grandest old-money folk live in one or two rooms in a wing because they can't afford the upkeep of these tumbledown piles. They're inherited burdens, a lot of these places. They've been passed on by their forefathers, who got rich during the days of the empire, and now there's a pressure to keep the jewels and paintings in the family, but actually these poor sods haven't got a pot to piss in. Or if they have, they're using it to catch the drips from the leaky ceiling, sure enough.'

'My heart bleeds for them. They should try living in a van for a bit.'

'And they're armed up to the eyeballs, a lot of them. Guns galore. Oh yes, they might have sold off the Titians and the Gainsboroughs, but they've held on to their duelling pistols and their muskets and they'll shoot anything with a pulse for the sport of it. And they dress scruffier than you.'

'Men of style, then.'

'This house beyond Cuckoo Spittle Meadows was definitely built with old lolly,' said Calvert. 'I crossed a few of them in my combat days. Dukes and the like. Some minor royals too. They were in the navy and air force, mainly. The sea and air is where they send the biggest troublemakers, you see, the doziest bastards or those who can't be trusted with the family wealth. It's mainly the second and third sons, you know, the ones set to inherit the crumbs from the cake rather than the cake itself. Often it's those who were kicked out of Eton and now need a bit of real discipline instilled in them, so they send them off to bob about on some far-flung sea where they're out the way, less likely to gamble away their fortunes or grope some poor young debutante in a West End cocktail bar and end up on the front page of the papers, the randy sods.'

Redbone shook his head in quiet compliance and Calvert continued, having clearly given the subject much thought over the years.

'One or two that I met had high-ranking uncles and godfathers who gave them a leg up past us plebs. Earls and lords and the like. They rarely made it into the SAS, though, because that was for the real kamikaze headcases who in civvy life would probably have been in jail or dead if they'd not found their vocation at a young age.'

'Like you?'

'Like me,' said Calvert. 'Anyway, the point is, we need to be extra-alert and have it away on our toes at the first sign of inter-lopers because, as you well know, my feral friend, the law always falls on the side of the poshos and not the peasants. No risks out there tomorrow.'

Redbone nodded. 'Agreed. We need to keep ourselves fit and free for the end-of-summer big one: the Honeycomb Double Helix. The last thing we want is to get collared now.'

An acquaintance of Redbone's, a small-time drug dealer with a limp and a boss-eyed whippet cross, entered the beer garden then and made a beeline for their table, so the plans he had drawn were hastily rolled away, and Redbone stood to greet him with a lot of mutual head-nodding and a handshake so elaborate it was a well-rehearsed piece of performance art in itself. To distract the interloper, Redbone steered him away from their conspiracy and over to the bar for pints of cider while Calvert basked in the last of the day's unbroken sun as it baked the drought-stricken land, idly daydreaming about the insanity of scale that would be the Cuckoo Spittle Name TBC, the violent fizz of his cold glass of ginger ale now dissipated into a sugary ticking sound, like a small incendiary device gripped in his grubby hand.

O

'Torches off.'

They turn off their lights and lean on the splintered old fence that marks the entrance to the fields that stretch before them, each thick with a barley crop that's ripe, rich and nearly ready for harvesting.

'What do you think of Cuckoo Spittle Thought Bubble?' Redbone says in a voice that is almost a whisper. 'It sounds like two worlds colliding – the natural and the scientific.'

'The instinctive and the intellectual.'

'Exactly.'

'It's perfect.'

The work is hard. The intricacy of the pattern and the steepness of the hill add extra miles and toil to a journey that is confined to one field yet feels as epic as a marathon. They tramp and gasp, sweat and flatten, and Calvert keeps having to consult Redbone in order to check that he is following the correct line and that the curves of the circles are as smooth and consistent as they can be. There is a lot of stopping and starting and quiet estimation of angles. Crossed ropes become entangled and the rough crop scratches at their arms. They itch all over and fail miserably to resist scratching away at their tormented skin.

Redbone offers to work on the 'head' of the caterpillar, the final bubble in the 'thought chain', which rests close to the top of the hill. He is rounding off the upper edge when he hears something behind him. A peal of laughter, then a voice. Or voices. Plural. They are followed by the sound of singing – a male voice, a soupy baritone that meanders away from the melody: *'Bring me my bow of burning gold, bring me my arrows of desire . . .'*

His fingers tighten their grip on the thin rope that has worn a callused groove across the palms of his hands. His boot moves an inch or two on the plank of wood underfoot, its grain displaying the scuff marks of a summer spent pressing the crop. The voice gets closer and Redbone looks around for Calvert so that he can signal to him to take cover, but the crop circle is so vast that he is out of sight.

'Bring me my spear, O clouds unfold! Bring me my chariot of fire . . . I say, there's one of our chaps.'

Redbone drops his rope and plank, and hunkers down. But it is too late. He has been spotted. He is instantly gripped with a sense of regret and failure. The code has been violated. Calvert would not have made the same mistake, and it is the disappointed look on his friend's face in the very near future that will be just as difficult to bear as the discovery of trespass itself.

Close by he hears the rustling of crops, the rattling of ears of barley. Then the voice again.

'Coo-ee.'

Redbone slowly stands, and there at the brow of the hill is a man a wearing a tuxedo, with a bow tie worn rakishly loose around the collar as if he has idly wandered straight from the film set of an adaptation of an E. M. Forster or Evelyn Waugh novel. Clinging to one arm is a young woman in an evening dress covered in sequins that sparkle in the moonlight. She is thin, her toned arms bare. In his other hand the man trails a bottle of champagne. The pulsing glow of a cigar stub radiates before him, as he puffs a plume of night-blue smoke.

'Hello there,' he says in a plummy voice, before adopting a pastiche of what Redbone takes to be a cockney working-class accent. 'Don't worry, we're not poaching nuffink for our pots, honest, guvnor.'

Aware of the vast crop circle behind him, Redbone walks towards the man and woman in an attempt to block their view. But they seem more interested in that which stands before them: a bedraggled young man, with wide eyes and a farmer's tan.

'Now, I know you're Hampton, but remind me, are you the younger or the elder?'

The man's accent is unavoidably aristocratic and his confidence and entitlement are heightened by veins full of sloshing booze that has settled in the dull puddles of his eyes, which appear to be a half-second behind the rest of his movements. They finally focus in on Redbone. He is from the big house and Redbone is surely on his land.

He improvises. Takes a guess.

'The younger.'

'Ah, that's what I thought. It's a terrific night to be out in it, is it not.'

The man is swaying on unsteady legs as he turns to the woman, who draws a strand of hair away from her face with her little finger. She has a long nose with narrow nostrils that somehow seem to perfectly match the shape of her eyes, which themselves give the impression that she is squinting into a strong headwind, even though the night is still. Or maybe her face, thinks Redbone, is that of someone who has just detected a disagreeable odour. She takes the measure of him in the manner of a person who has certainly never known fear when a good brandy and a good barrister is all one needs in life.

'Hampton the Younger,' the man says by way of explanation to her, as he gestures towards Redbone. 'Damn good gamekeeper. His family has worked the estate for decades, isn't that right?'

'Oh yes,' says Redbone. 'A long time, sir.'

The 'sir' tastes sour in Redbone's mouth but is an addition he feels is necessary given the circumstances. The aristocrat has a puffy face that suggests gluttony, though his frame is actually rather slender. His jet-black hair is gelled back tight against his head and has a sheen to it, but a few tufts have broken free on the sides and stick out now at absurd angles, like the ruffled feathers of a bathing crow. His face is like that of a child's drawing – two eyes, a nose and a mouth drawn onto a pink balloon – and there is something familiar about him. Redbone wonders if he is a politician or one of those colourful minor royals that Calvert mentioned, those comical throwbacks to England's colonial past who somehow manage to perennially hold positions of power and high status despite their obvious ineptitude, highly suspect political opinions or indeed lack of proximity to the real world. Only then does Redbone realise who the man resembles: the moon. Yes, he has the same lustrous, cherub-cheeked face that he observed back on the first night at Alton Kellett.

'Any action tonight?' he asks.

Redbone shakes his head, wondering how long this case of mistaken identity can be maintained.

'It's quiet.'

'You're damn right it is,' says the aristocrat. 'Any poachers would be most unwise to tackle you and your boys.'

Then, turning to the woman, he explains, 'Some of these rotters rustle our pheasants and rabbits and sell them to the markets, you know. They think we don't know but we do. Once they did it out of poverty but now a lot of them do it for the sport, you know, to have one over the toffs. Oh yes. And that makes it worse, in a way. Down in the village they'll tell you all about it, I'm sure. A splenetic bunch, some of them. As rum as you like. Centuries they've been trying to lift our birds and game, and centuries we've been catching them at it. It's a battle of wits, really. Cat and mouse. Isn't that right, Holbeck?'

'Hampton,' says Redbone.

'What?'

'I was just saying my name's Hampton, sir.'

The man in the tuxedo looks first confused, then affronted.

'Well, *of course* it is.'

He takes a swig from his bottle and then puffs on his cigar, but, seeing that it has gone out, scowls and tosses it aside. Tosses it into the dry, drought-ridden tinderbox that is his own crop.

'Having a bit of a do down at the house,' he says to Redbone. 'A few of the lads got a bit out of hand, so I thought I'd step out and get a bit of air with this one. Show her the family spread, so to speak.'

With one arm around her waist, he pulls the woman close to him in a vulgar display of ownership.

'Thought I'd show her the old place from up here. It really is the best vantage point.'

'Yes, it's a nice spot,' says Redbone, nervous that Calvert might appear from the crop behind them at any point, though, knowing him, his friend will already have read the situation and be well hidden from view. And possibly even listening from close by.

Only then does the woman speak. 'You don't look much like a gamekeeper.'

She too sounds intoxicated, though more a slurred mess of pills than alcohol; Redbone has always prided himself on being able to recognise the different chemical highs and lows within people. And this one is a pill popper, no question. She's rattling like a bottle of grasshoppers.

'And what exactly do you think a gamekeeper looks like, Tiggy?'

The posh man, who Redbone has surmised is definitely either the owner of the big house or the son of the owner, for it is difficult to gauge the age of someone whose face has probably looked around fifty since he hit puberty, winks at Redbone, as if inviting him in on the ribbing of his female companion.

She considers the question for a moment.

'Sort of gout-stricken, and sporting a deerstalker hat?'

The man guffaws at this.

'Deerstalkers are for those who stalk the deer, dear. And that's usually up in the Highlands. Besides which, it's the 1980s, not the 1880s. Gamekeepers can wear whatever the hell they like so long as they do the job, isn't that right, Frampton?'

Redbone shrugs and nods. Though he is enjoying the deceit, he wants to get the conversation over with quickly. To abandon a night's work at this stage would be a major setback, but can they risk continuing, having been spotted in the area – and will this moon-faced, balloon-headed sot even remember their encounter when he sobers up? As the aristocrat takes another swig from the bottle and passes it to the woman, Redbone sneaks a glance over his shoulder. Miraculously, from this angle the Cuckoo Spittle Thought Bubble is not visible. They are too close to the crop, and the field too sharply angled, to get a clear view upon the night's work. That it is as dark as it will get – which is to say not that dark at all – also helps.

The woman, Tiggy, takes a long two-handed gulp, and after a self-satisfied belch says, 'When you catch a poacher' – but she does not finish the sentence.

Her companion not only completes the question, but answers it for Redbone too. 'When he catches a poacher he gives him a bloody good walloping, don't you?'

Redbone, who naturally is on the side of the poacher, shrugs and wonders whether his integrity and attitude towards the class system will allow him to be any more ingratiating to this balloon than he already has been. Then he remembers Calvert might be listening close by.

'Well, sometimes we do like to give them a sporting chance, sir.'

'A sporting chance how?' asks the woman – Tiggy – and Balloon-Head seems interested in the response too.

'Yes, how?'

'Well,' says Redbone, as intrigued as they are as to what he might say next. He hears the words come out of his mouth. 'We like to give them a head start. We send them off into the woods or the crop, you see, and loudly give them to the count of five. It's only fair.'

'Then what?' says Tiggy.

'Yes,' says Balloon-Head. 'Then what?'

'Well, it depends. Sometimes we'll set the dogs after them, maybe to tear a muscle or two off a leg or an arm, and other times we'll take a few potshots.'

At this, the woman's eyes widen, but she appears excited too.

'You *shoot* them?'

'Not fatally. We never aim for their heads.'

'Where, then?'

'Yes,' says Balloon-Head again, pausing with the bottle raised halfway to his mouth, 'where, then, by Christ?'

Redbone hesitates, savouring the suspense he has improvised with surprising ease and imagination.

'Crikey,' she urges. 'Do tell.'

'Oh, you know, sir. The fleshy parts, mainly.'

'Such as?'

'I'm sure you can imagine,' says Redbone, warming to the subject. 'Anything that's flapping or dangling, really. It's the least they deserve. I mean, they're a terrible work-shy lot, the most of them. Dole-scrounging peasants who've never done a day's toil in their lives, while the taxes of good people like yourselves keep them in fast food and pornography. Scum, that's what they are. Underclass scum.'

'Here, here,' says the aristocrat. 'The flappers or the danglers indeed. Good man.'

'But *you've* never done a day's work in your life either, Xander.'

Redbone suppresses a smile. His face aches from trying to keep the smirk at bay. *Xander*, he thinks. He'd have not lasted two minutes at my school.

'Running this place is more work than you could imagine,' Xander replies, once again indignant, a look that Redbone can see comes easily to him. 'I can't even begin to tell you, because I know you wouldn't be able to take it all in. Anyway, perhaps you could tell Holbeck here what it is that you do?'

'I'm an actor,' says Tiggy.

'Yes, she is an ac-*tor*,' he says to Redbone. 'Do you recognise her?'

He hesitates.

'I –'

'No you do not, because my darling acquaintance here is resting, and just happens to be one of the very best in her field. At resting, that is.'

'Xander, you sod.'

Redbone moves from one foot to the other, desperate for the inane conversation to be over. It seems only a matter of time before this pair, as drunk as they may be, finally see through his pretence and set the dogs on him, only theirs won't be imaginary.

'Here, old chap,' says Xander, 'a question before we depart for a swift moonlit dip in the lake: have you ever come across any of these crop circles about the place?'

'Crop . . . circles?' says Redbone as the second word catches in his dry throat and turns into a cough.

'Yes, you know – strange patterns in the corn.'

'I can't say I have, no. And strictly speaking this isn't corn, sir.'

'But you know the things I mean?'

'I'm not sure I do.'

'They're all over the news, man. There's talk of unknown entities – aliens, that type of thing. It's all highly mysterious.'

'Aliens?' says Tiggy. 'Here?'

'Quite possibly.'

'In Wiltshire?'

'Yes, dear. In Wiltshire.'

'How exciting. Can we go and look for them?'

'What, now? Of course not. We're going for a starkers dip, remember?'

'But isn't it cold?'

Ignoring her, Xander pats down his pockets, searching for something. From inside his jacket he pulls out two cigars. 'Here you are, Brompton. Have one of these. They're offensively decent.'

Redbone takes the cigar from him. 'Thank you, sir.'

Xander waves away the false gratitude as Redbone slides the cigar behind one ear. Tiggy drains the rest of the bottle and then launches it through the air, into the crop. It lands in one of the unseen thought bubbles with a *thunk*.

'Bit reckless,' sniffs Xander.

'Oh, loosen up, you stiff,' she says, turning on uncertain legs and heading back over the hill towards the house.

Xander's eyes follow her rear for a moment, then he raises an eyebrow at Redbone, and wedges the cigar in the corner of his mouth.

'Well, best press on. You'll let me know if you see any, though, won't you?'

'Poachers?' says Redbone, adding a distinctly more sarcastic-sounding 'Sir?'

'No, these crop circles. I reckon they could be a real money-spinner for the estate were one to turn up. Some of the farms are raking it in, apparently.'

Redbone doesn't know whether to feel exhilarated or deflated by this thought.

'Yes. Yes, I will.'

'Good man. You can find me up at the house – any time. But you know that already.'

He turns to leave, then hesitates. His eyes seem to search his thoughts for the correct words.

'If you could keep mum about seeing Tiggy up here, there's a good fellow. She's betrothed to another, as am I, so best to keep it . . .' He taps the side of nose. 'Well, you know.'

Winking, Redbone taps the side of his nose too. 'We all have our secrets.'

Xander leaves and disappears over the crest of the hill once again, whistling 'Jerusalem'.

'*Tosser.*'

His head reappears. 'What's that?'

'I said, "Night, sir."'

'Night, Timpson.'

○

Two minutes pass before Calvert makes himself known with a short, curt hiss.

'*Psssst.*'

Redbone looks around, yet sees nothing except the silhouette of stalks leaning away from the warm westerly breeze that advents the coming dayspring.

'*Psssst.* Over here.'

'It's alright,' says Redbone. 'They've gone.'

Not more than ten feet away Calvert's head slowly appears above the crop. In him, Redbone sees the SAS soldier that once was. He stands up, brushes dirt from his clothes and then examines his elbows.

'That bottle could have brained me,' he says. 'Good job I've got good reactions.'

'Did you hear all that?'

'Some of it. The tail end. I was down the hill but crawled all the way up just to make sure you weren't blowing our cover entirely. My arms are killing me – look at that.'

On his bare elbows and forearms are red-raw streaks from where he has partially skinned himself while dragging his body through the arid dirt. Like a snail, thinks Redbone. Like a worm.

'I thought I did rather well,' he says.

'Do you know who that was you were talking to?'

'Little Lord Fauntleroy there? It was Xander from the big house and his undernourished Lady Di-wannabe mistress.'

'Well, yes,' says Calvert. 'Earl William Lachlan Alexander Bruce Lascar of Winchem, son of the Duke of Winchem, who is also known as the Earl of Maidenstoke, Baron Jutland and several other titles besides. When his old man pops off, Xander there will be the third-biggest landowner in Britain. His father is the man the Queen goes to when she's a bit short on cash. He'll probably be running the country one day, if he can keep his dick in his pants.'

'Christ alive, he certainly seemed thick enough. He thought I was the gamekeeper.'

'So I gathered. Have you ever played anyone in a production?'

'Only the fool,' says Redbone. 'Come on, let's get this finished.'

O

By midday on Sunday, Cuckoo Spittle Meadows is busy with photographers, journalists, agency stringers, a 'cerealogist' advocating several conflicting paranormal explanations for the crop circle's creation, excited UFOlogists, the local MP, a Catholic priest there in his 'official capacity' as 'demonic exorcist', a man waggling primitive dowsing rods, a disgraced psychic, two Romany gypsy women selling blessed corn dollies, a helicopter pilot eating a packed lunch, an MI5 representative, a class of student meteorologists from Exeter, a retired physicist explaining to anyone passing that the pattern was created by an 'electro-magnetic-hydrodynamic plasma vortex', a grand wizard who has arrived from Cornwall, a New Age a cappella vocal group improvising a work that will later feature on their album *Lapsed Eden / Visions of Gaia*, several leading Greenpeace activists, a man with a van selling teas, coffees and bacon sandwiches, a very hung-over and confused-looking Earl William Lachlan Alexander Bruce Lascar of Winchem, four police officers, half-a-dozen dogs, and Brian Eno.

Their cars cram the passing places and line the lane down which Redbone and Calvert departed in darkness just hours ago. And now they trample roughshod all over the pictogram, damaging the crop as they mindlessly snap the bone-dry stalks and spoil the fine detailing of Redbone and Calvert's artwork while they take samples of barley, wave various dubious-looking home-made devices over the crop and let their yapping hounds hunch over and indiscriminately evacuate their backs wherever they feel compelled to do so.

At home in his tiny house Calvert presses RECORD on his VHS player and adds news footage of Cuckoo Spittle Thought Bubble shot from overhead this afternoon. It joins his compilation of clips – it is the only time he uses his television – and then, when the news item is over, he turns off the TV, switches off the lights and sits in the dark, his forearms and elbows sore, his scalp itching and his limbs heavy from the exertion of creating something colossal.

Something beyond.

Visitors have flocked to farmland on the vast Wiltshire country estate belonging to the 7th Duke of Winchem to see a crop circle that appeared there on Sunday morning. The intricate pattern, which has been dubbed the Cuckoo Spittle Thought Bubble in honour of the hill on which it has appeared, measures 450 feet in length and has attracted hundreds of people.

The duke was not in residence, though his son, Earl Alexander of Winchem, 31, was on hand to greet all-comers. 'I wish I could say that I witnessed flying saucers full of little green men armed with ray guns,' commented Earl Winchem, 'but I didn't. I had just returned to the family home entirely alone for a quiet weekend of rest and reflection, and to put a few personal affairs in order, and neither saw nor heard any activity overnight that might be deemed suspicious or untoward. When I awoke bright and early I was as stunned as anyone to discover what was here on our doorstep. This is surely the work of a shadowy set of dusk devils of unknown origins or motives. I have been up in the chopper this morning and what I will say is, whoever created this thing made a bloody good effort of it. It's art and if I could frame it and hang it, I would. More of it, I say. More of it.'

The *Guardian*,
4 August 1989

THROSTLE HENGE ASTEROID NECKLACE

England is thirsty. The land lies dry, parched.

The cloudless sky is a headstand in a swimming pool, aqua-blue.

Across the south it has not rained for weeks and the golden plains begin to take on the look of a desert as certain crops – corn, maize, those vegetables of a more delicate disposition – tilt and wither or shrivel into themselves as they draw upon their last reserves. Some die right there in their holes. The vast grasslands have passed the point of purpose; the usual temperate climate of regular sunshine and short showers that helps turn grass into vital protein for the grazing animals has been imbalanced to such an extent that the production of silage that is used to feed the region's livestock over the coming months will now be the worst it has been in decades. Naturally, milk and beef production will suffer as a result. The autumn's apple harvest will be poor also, with the majority of varieties dry and undersized, the yield greatly depleted. The same with pears too. In two months' time cider and perry presses will sit largely unused, gathering dust for another winter.

The south-west region of England usually produces more food annually than all of Scotland and twice as much as Wales, but not this year.

Not this year, when the skin of the land tightens and cracks and all creatures descend on those few scattered bodies of water and slow-flowing streams that have not yet dried up entirely. Dehydration furtively forces shy nocturnal creatures out into the open, and a simple village pond fed from a wellspring is now as precious as an oasis in the Gobi. The sun-softened roads become littered with the flattened, smeared corpses of hedgehogs, badgers and deer, killed in their search for water, their entrails mingling with the gluey black bitumen. The still air smells of oil.

Rabbits bake in the airless cellars of the earth. The sky croaks a brief eulogy in only the faintest of breezes.

The oilseed rape too is in decline, its vast fields having been harvested since mid-July, and soon it will be entirely gone for another year. The blinding yellow tide that has washed across the county and dazzled all who cast their eyes upon it as they passed by in cars, its scent filling the air with a sour honey odour that proves intoxicating to some, but whose bitter, stringent tang is repulsive to others, is now in full retreat. Yet the lingering pungent smell of the intensively grown plant almost has a physicality to it that can still be tasted. It is like chewing on cotton wool, and it tightens the chests of asthmatics who inhale it too deeply. Viewed through the liquid-like haze of a mirage, the very last few surviving oilseed stems that sag in thin clusters are so bright they appear almost unreal, though the distant church spires that earlier in the season became lost in the vivid ocean of it now emerge in the landscape once more. The luminescence of early summer is now kept alive in the hot-lava light displays and the glowsticks, the T-shirts and the bandanas of the acid-tripping party crews who illegally gather across such southern counties each weekend to dance their way to delirium in these clandestine corners.

All living things are connected between seed and sod, and sod and sky, and when one component in the chain of production is altered, ailing or inefficient the entire ecosystem suffers. It is not enough just to produce oilseed rape, even in surplus, and the wheat fields whisper their desperate thirst. The barley meadows dream of better days. Lethargic cows swat at flies that gather at the saline pools of their eyes with whiplike tails, and tick-stricken sheep seek the corners where hedgerows cast short shadows, masticating with urgency.

And the worms lie slow-squirming into expiration beneath the noonday sun.

○

In his tiny house Calvert sits early on a Saturday morning with the curtains closed and the windows open, and watches as first a wasp and then a bee passes through.

His mind feels like a furnace and he fights to immolate old bad memories that have surfaced like fossils during indolent hours. To do so he focuses on the angry hum of the wasp, the fuller buzz of the furred bee. He watches as they bat against wall and window, two trapped explorers on a temporary diversion, their wide worlds shrunken down, as is his.

As other familiar noises fill his room – the rattle of the milk van, the incessant chatter of passing children, wood pigeons on the chimney stack – he thinks about the nights he and Redbone have spent out in the fields so far this season, each in its own way more thrilling than a roller-coaster ride, and how, although the thought of having to abandon Longbarrow Whale still niggles him, at least Cuckoo Spittle Thought Bubble was a triumph achieved in the face of near adversity. And he thinks of the next one, and the next one and the one after that, as a means to avoid his mind turning to past traumas that stalk his every waking moment.

Bare-chested in his armchair and perspiring in the half-light, he plans in great detail the night-ops strategies required to create something that will far exceed anything they have done to date and push their ambition and abilities to their very limits: the Honeycomb Double Helix. To do so he has researched the area, extensively reading up on land ownership, local history and mythology. He has pored over maps and borrowed books, and will continue to do so. His methodology, he knows, is sound, even if the dents in his mind need panel-beating back into shape now and again. '*Dum spiro spero*,' he whispers to the empty room.

Redbone's old VW meanwhile becomes a brazier, a mobile hot box. He keeps moving it around a network of safe stopping places where he can rest up away from intrusion and sit with the windows and doors open without worrying too much about thieves: picnic spots, old quarries reclaimed by nature, riverside locations.

Here he works through the night on the Honeycomb Double Helix and sees himself as a sole spelunker exploring the deepest caverns in the dank tunnels of his imagination. Sometimes, upon waking, it all feels so real he can hear the slow existential *drip-drip* of lonely water onto lonely rock, and only the heat and the bright midday sun tell him otherwise.

When he is not working he tinkers with musical ideas on his bass guitar, which has two strings that struggle to stay in tune, but he is listless, and forever in search of fresh cool corners in which to park up, preferably near flowing water so that he can bathe and bask naked and wash his clothes, and then lie watching them as they steam dry on the grass in the mid-afternoon glare.

Wherever he goes, his spare pair of trousers and various T-shirts – most of them advertising obscure hardcore punk bands that he once considered friends, rivals and contemporaries and who have long since split up – hang drying from branches and hedges. When fatigue finally falls upon him he bunches two pillows and makes a sandwich of his skull. Then, as he sleeps, forgettable dreams drill through the centre of his troubled slumber. They are nonsensical narratives played out in broken, jerking motions like the magic-lantern light shows of old.

Redbone and Calvert are both distracted and the drought makes everything hard work, but the season's mission is all-consuming now; they are sun-drunk on their own secret project, and when they are not out crafting and grafting they are thinking about it. Separated and out of contact for days, they each reflect on the brilliant beauty of the Thought Bubble over at Cuckoo

Spittle Meadows, and the attention it has garnered, while working out ways to improve upon it in the next one. Because the next one is always a beacon, beaming hope across the strange and haunted landscapes of their solitary existences.

The long dry days and short hot nights somehow heighten their individual personality attributes and defects too, as everything else beyond the next circle – the banal details of their day-to-day existences, for example – grows increasingly futile. Deep down, they know that the summer has a limit and their venture is restricted by a time frame. At some point the calendar will make an enemy of them and Calvert especially does not want to think beyond the season. In his mind, autumn sits like a headstone in a cemetery that he dares not enter.

In the meantime, sleep for both men becomes broken and fitful, birdsong their daily alarm. They cling to the idea of the next one.

They nourish and nurture it. They need it.

○

Perhaps it is because there is going to be an eclipse tonight that both Redbone and Calvert individually detect an extra charge in the air, as if they have chugged too much strong coffee, or are a little jet-lagged, or have been up for days.

Or perhaps it is because Throstle Henge is a sacred stone circle whose ancient sarsens sit within plain view of the chosen field at which they arrive in late evening, during full daylight. The heat of their respective abodes, and a powerful compulsion to create, means they have arrived earlier than usual, glad to be out of the house, the van.

Though comprised of a dozen standing stones that are not particularly huge in scale, Throstle Henge is one of the best-preserved

Neolithic sites in the country. It is also believed to have been constructed at the converging point of several ley lines, and therefore is an internationally renowned place of historic and spiritual importance and a popular destination for those who are dissuaded by the sanitised visitor experience of Stonehenge or the crowds of Avebury. Throstle Henge is for the slightly more discerning stone circle fan, and requires a little more effort than simply stepping out of an air-conditioned coach and snapping a few photos to experience its mystical glory.

That the mystery of exactly who constructed such a circle, and why, still endures to this day, continues to divide the opinions of experts who study prehistoric Britain, and lends Throstle Henge an extra layer of intrigue. Everything about its origins is speculative, its secrets awaiting future excavation. Really, no one knows anything of its true purpose.

To work near such a site, especially at this time of the year, is a big risk, so they must be diligent and swift in their markings.

Calvert says as much.

'We must be diligent in our markings. And swift.'

Redbone, whose hearing has been damaged by a decade of standing next to big speakers in small rooms, and who is also prone to slipping into mental zones that render him detached from the moment, does not hear him, though.

'What? Did you say something?'

'Never mind.'

○

As evening falls like an Oxford blue sheet across the rolling dusty land, Redbone and Calvert first take a walk around the stone circle. They run their rough hands over coarse stone that is still warm from the day's direct sunlight. They feel the past held within them and press fingers into the same holes probed by their forefathers five thousand years ago, and they wonder at the stories the stones might tell could they speak. The things they have seen.

It is not the stones they are interested in, however, but the view from them, for even an amateur fan knows that most significant Neolithic monuments such as Throstle Henge were strategically constructed on landmarks or elevations in order for them to be seen from great distances. They were their own advertisements for whatever activity once took place there. Whether they were markets for trading, or used for purposes altogether more nefarious, such as fertility rituals, births and burials, or human sacrifice, stone circles could be seen by people across the plains, their view unimpeded by the trees or hills, or more recently the buildings, housing estates, retail parks or motorways of the modern world, which might now lie in the way.

The sunset this evening is spectacular, the sky a scree of fleshy pinks and fiery oranges as both men watch in wordless wonder.

The last chattering notes of bird calls become infrequent, until finally there is nothing but the gaps between them, and those gaps take the shape of long silence that settles the nerves and cools the blood.

From up here they can see the location for the night's work, two fields over.

From up here they can also see that beneath the skin of the earth is the curve of its skull. It is the foundation upon on which all life sits. Worms crawl from the fissures in the skull to turn the earth that is the skin. The worms of England. They convert death and decay into the composted soil from which all plants and trees and crops grow. All creatures have one true purpose and this is theirs, just as for Redbone and Calvert it is making crop circles, and nothing else.

Throstle Henge Asteroid Necklace is a largely circular design, but one surrounded by an external necklace or 'asteroid belt' of dozens of small circles, like pearls strung around a neck. Redbone points out the key areas of his design that require particular attention – where parabola curves must meet right-angled corners, and adjacent circles' circumferences must nearly meet but, crucially, never overlap. Within the main design are also more circles, laid in such a way as to suggest planets orbiting a central sun. And just to further complicate matters, whereas a normal design is drawn *into* the crop, Redbone has tonight included several further fine necklace lines made from standing wheat whose creation requires very precise measurements and a delicate touch. Gone is the rampant wholesale trampling of crops in these areas, and instead sections of it must now be almost sculpted, their beauty and power defined by the absence of the flattened wheat around them. It is an exercise in precision and control.

Calvert looks at the sky. 'Will we even have time?'

'I've done some calculations,' says Redbone. 'If we get down there and start in the next twenty minutes and work without a break, we should be done by dawn.'

'We need to keep our eyes open in case there are any midnight lurkers visiting the stones. You can see everything from here. We'll be completely exposed.'

'True. But we've not been caught yet.'

'There's the eclipse to think of too.'

'I'm prepared to take the risk if you are.'

'"Risk" is not a word I usually like,' says Calvert.

'But you were in the SAS.'

'I was, and there was plenty of risk involved in all our opera-tions. But the risks were calculated as best they could be, which is the only way to decrease adverse results when entering unfamiliar territory. You could say risk was mitigated by advance intel.'

'A bit like this.'

'Well, a bit.'

'What's the worst that can happen?'

Calvert considers the question.

'Well, they'll never catch us. They might see us, but they'll never catch us. No way. That won't happen. I won't let it. Not on my watch.'

'So the worst thing that can happen would be another design abandoned. Just like the Longbarrow Whale.'

They both think about that night again now, and the frus-tration of leaving an incomplete work. They remember too the fly-tippers of Alton Kellett back in May and tiny bubbles of anger burst within them.

Calvert shakes his head. 'That's not happening either. I've never seen anything like the Throstle Henge Asteroid Necklace before. No one will have; over on the plains of Wyoming and Oklahoma they're still stuck doing standard circles. Amateurs, rank amateurs. I'm almost embarrassed for them. We have to make the dream a reality. We need to bring it into being. We must.'

'Then we shall.'

O

They wait until it is only just dark enough for the standing stones to become flattened into simple featureless blocks pressed against the landscape behind them, and a scratchy pall has settled over the field. The veil of night. Then they begin.

Even now the moon appears especially bright, as if it knows an eclipse is coming and is summoning all its strength to partake in a spectacular display.

Redbone and Calvert are about to descend the mound that hosts the stone circle and immerse themselves in the gilt-coloured crop, which at its deepest has grown to shoulder height, when there is movement behind them. They turn and look down the slope and one field over, which has been left fallow this year in order to follow the old practices of crop rotation, as a convoy of vehicles enters the dry rutted pasture of stubble. There is something unnerving about the way seven cars and a van snake across the land, their headlights off, and then park in a circle, each facing inwards.

Only then do they turn on their lights, and the men – and they are all men – climb out from their cars. Each vehicle seems to hold more bodies than expected and even from this distance Redbone and Calvert can see that there is a collective energy to their movements and a sense of purpose to the way in which they assemble themselves into two opposing camps.

The headlights cast long shadows that appear grotesque as they loom and bend, their elongated limbs distended. The cars create an over-bright ring, an illuminated area, and in that arena the assembled men are restless. Even from this distance, the tension is visible. The sound of short laughter rises up through the night to reach Redbone and Calvert up at the stones as the men gather in huddles, then break away and reconfigure into other huddles that look conspiratorial. There is much conferring.

'Some wild scene,' murmurs Redbone. 'I wonder what's transpiring.'

Calvert chews the inside of his cheek.

'I don't know. But I'd wager big money it's nothing good.'

One man takes the centre of the circle and addresses the others, but Redbone and Calvert cannot make out what he says. Instead they see gestures distorted in the flare of the dipped beams.

Then from either side of the small crowd two men appear. They stride determinedly into the circle and one of them peels off his top to reveal a bare torso, as white as the seam of chalk that runs beneath Salisbury Plain. The other has a vest on, and both are wearing loose trackie trousers and trainers.

'Gypsies,' says Calvert.

'Do you think?'

'I know. Could be didicois or could be Irish travellers, it's hard to tell from here. It's a prizefight, though. They're all laying bets on them.'

'But why here, why now?'

'The same reason we're here right now. Because they can't or don't want to belong. Because they don't want to be disturbed.'

Without ceremony or introduction, the two men square off and begin to punch one another, almost casually at first, and then more frantically. They come together in a clinch as a single entity, a two-headed shifting, snorting beast, but the most unnerving thing is that the crowd does not make a noise as it might be expected to. They merely observe in silence; or any encouragement that is proffered is done so quietly that it does not reach Redbone and Calvert up on the mound. They can hear only the sounds of slapping skin and bone on bone, and the occasional grunt rising up from somewhere deep within, and that makes Redbone think of a bull in a field or drunken punks slamming together in a circle pit, and Calvert of smashing the face of a scared Argentinian man-child with the butt of his gun until something broke beneath, so irrevocably damaged as to be beyond repair.

'This is ugly,' says Redbone. 'It's primitive.'

'It is,' says Calvert. 'But it's also consensual. At least there's some sort of a moral code involved.'

'Is there?'

'Of sorts. What you're witnessing is an age-old tradition. Either they're fighting for the sport of it or they're settling an inter-family feud. Think of it this way: cockerels and dogs don't have a say, but at least these lads do. It's not war. No one has been conscripted.'

The two men clinch and separate again and move round one another in a clockwise motion. More punches are thrown; the wilder ones miss, but others connect.

'I'm glad we're up here and not down there,' says Redbone.

Calvert does not reply. They watch for half a minute longer.

'I'm glad we can't see the blood.'

O

A little after 3 a.m. the atmosphere around them changes as the moon enters the earth's umbra and then slowly passes through the centre of it. Agitated birds start singing too early but then in their confusion fall silent once more.

A dark crescent spreads like a silent malevolent force across the mottled greys and whites of the sullen moon's countenance, its surface a curious patina.

Redbone and Calvert stop what they are doing and stare upwards until their necks ache, not daring to drag their eyes away from the empyrean display. The blank clock-like face fades from view as the black shutter of the earth's shadow covers it to create a total lunar eclipse, and for a few seconds it feels as if the darkness will be unending and absolute. Momentarily the land is an undeveloped photograph and time is rendered meaningless, and both Redbone and Calvert are aware that they are part of a long lineage of men and women who have stood in these very fields in rapt astonishment for thousands of years, infatuated and intrigued by the magic of the sky at night, and feeling the smallness of their lives and the preciousness of their planetary home.

But the moment is only fleeting, for then the shadows retreat and the light reverts to the deep blueness of an August night, and the recharged moon is bright. Still confused, the birds strike up dozens of bepuzzled conversations with one another.

Redbone and Calvert stoop and trample onwards and the Throstle Henge Asteroid Necklace expands across the landscape, a fallen galaxy in miniature. Up above from the hill, the stones watch on and their silhouettes look like the forms of people frozen in a solemn ritual to an ancient unknown god who died long ago.

Beyond them, only stars.

O

Driving back still in darkness they pull into a long layby where during the day there is a burger van but tonight there is only a rubbish bin overflowing with twisted cans and fast-food cartons, and two cars pulled over, and just beyond them in the cover of the bushes a woman is bent over and she has a man at each end and another is standing off to one side watching, and the glare of the lights of Redbone's van dazzles them, and four faces turn almost mechanically to look their way, four flat faces as blank as plates squinting into the blinding whiteness as Redbone and Calvert pass, four surprised masks, and they do not stop, instead they keep driving past them and Redbone says, 'Odd night', and Calvert says, 'Double-odd night indeed', and Redbone says, 'Maybe the moon has a strange effect on people', and Calvert replies, 'Yes, yes, it definitely does', and the old VW eats up the road, chews on the miles, its old engine growling and belching as they drive a hole on through towards morning.

Either PAGAN WEIRDOS are RUNNING AMOK in the countryside or Blighty has been INVADED BY ALIENS this summer. How else can we explain the strange crop circles in fields all across England's green and pleasant land? IRATE FARMERS have complained to authorities about the destruction of their wheat fields after the MYSTERIOUS PATTERNS have appeared with increasing regularity over the past few months. At least little green men in their UFOs make a change from RANDY MILKMAIDS BONKING in the hay bales. Bring back National Service, we say!

The *Sun*, 18 August 1989

UNTITLED
(BRONZE FOX MANDALA)

And still no rain does fall.

Not a lone maverick drop of it.

Redbone spends much of his time drinking home-brewed cider. The heat has made him feel anxious, and the anxiety can only be kept at bay by alcohol. The fizzy cider is the leftover dregs from a bad batch and fills him with so much gas that his body creaks and groans like an ice floe. But still he swallows it down from bottles that he floats in streams to keep cool. He ties them with string to a branch pegged into the bankside, or hides them in little underwater cromlechs of stacked stones, but it is never quite cold enough and at night his dreams are like a stomach ache of the mind.

Belches come from his mouth like blank cartoon speech bubbles awaiting words.

He thinks of himself as an iceberg often, in order to cool his broiling mind.

Calvert does not have cider, and is still not even tempted by the prospect of it. Cider is not good for him, nor is beer or vodka or whiskey – especially whiskey; alcohol remains the sniper that can take him out at any time if he is not vigilant. It took him six months of civilian life and too many A&E nights having glass picked from his knuckles and gravel from his lips, his trousers torn and flapping at the knees, to learn this, and his resolve remains strong. Never again will he be seen directing traffic topless on a roundabout island. Never again will he fight a litter bin. His abstinence is a lifetime commitment.

Instead he keeps the windows open and the curtains shut, and as they billow and flap he lifts weights and eats a lot of slices of cold, crisp watermelon. He walks around his tiny house in his underpants, spitting the melon pips into an empty coal bucket, sucking ice cubes and listening to classical music on the radio. It soothes him. Occasionally he watches his recorded collection of news clips of their greatest crop circle creations with the sound turned off. These too soothe him.

Crescents of rotting watermelon rind gather in his flip-top bin, and more wasps arrive.

He knows something is wrong when Redbone turns up late outside the pub in his VW, looking bleary-eyed and more bedraggled than usual. Calvert climbs in and they drive out of the village. They don't say anything for some time.

'Well, you look like a sack of crap,' says Calvert finally, 'without the sack.'

'Thanks, pal.'

'What's wrong?'

'Nothing,' replies Redbone, not taking his eyes off the road. 'Nothing's wrong.'

Calvert looks at him and Redbone feels like his head is a soup tureen into which his friend has plunged his hand and is rooting around for something solid, something tangible.

'Will you stop that.'

'Stop what?'

'Trying to read my mind.'

'I know there must be something wrong because you're not talking. And you're always talking. Also, you look like you're out on day release.'

'My mind's a little fried, Ivan, that's all,' says Redbone. 'Too much adult apple juice.'

'That's all?'

Redbone sighs and then shrugs. 'Well, if you really want to know, I just sometimes wonder if it's all worth it.'

'You're tired. You're tired because you've been working on the Bronze Fox Mandala non-stop.'

Redbone scrunches up one eye, scratches his scalp and looks away across the fields.

'Actually, I've been drunk for days. Besides, it's not work if you love it.'

'That's true, but it's you that is doing the real work here: you're digging deep into your subconscious to conceive this stuff. The candle of your imagination has been burned from both ends, whereas I just gather intel and do half the heavy lifting. I'm the map-man, the practical thinker. I acknowledge that. From each according to his ability and all that.'

'You're quoting Karl Marx now?'

'Yes. Also, of course, you're effectively homeless.'

'You call it homeless,' counters Redbone. 'I call it free.'

They drive onwards. Both their windows are open and the evening air smells of sherbet and pollen, wet dogs and sewage.

'I think it's the Honeycomb Double Helix,' Redbone finally says.

'What about it?'

'I just can't seem to leave it alone. Or it won't leave me alone. It's there, always, blocking the sun. It's inside me now. It's like a tapeworm squirming through my innards. Even in sleep it's there. And I do sometimes wonder.'

'Wonder what?'

'Whether it is worth it. The toll it takes on the rest of my life.'

Calvert removes his sunglasses and looks at Redbone. He has worn the shades for so long that the shape of them is visible in the lighter skin that the sun has not tanned behind them, leaving a raccoon-like eye mask and a deep imprint that sits on the bridge of his nose too. But it is the eyes themselves that Redbone really notices. They are penetratingly blue. Surprisingly so. And they seem to be ever-changing, from teal to turquoise, cerulean to sapphire to cobalt. Redbone thinks that with those eyes his friend could do absolutely anything he wants in life. But also, with eyes that striking, it's little wonder he keeps them covered, for they could draw unwanted attention too. And then it occurs to him that perhaps Calvert *is* doing exactly what he wants in life, and in a way maybe he himself is as well, and this thought lifts his spirits slightly. All of this he gets from a rare but powerful glimpse at his friend's eyes. He has to force himself to look back to the road.

'Listen,' says Calvert emphatically. 'These circles, fractals, knots, ropes, clocks, locks, keys, ribbons, dolphins, whales, whirlpools and mandalas that you design are many things to many people. They are part of a wordless story that goes beyond language barriers to become metaphor for some, myth for others, and a mystery to most except us. They tell a strange story, create a narrative. More than anything, they are something to believe in during cynical times. Who knows if humans are even going to make it to the twenty-first century, but belief breeds hope and hope is essential. That's something that has taken me many years and too much heavy stuff to finally come to understand. Hope is essential. Hope is the human currency, and we're spreading it about.'

'Then they'd surely hate us if they knew we were responsible for these hoaxes,' says Redbone. 'They'll want to lynch us.'

'Hoaxes?' says Calvert, with the slightest flinty flash of anger in his eyes; anger that the sunglasses otherwise usually keep hidden. 'Who said anything about hoaxes? Not me. No, no, not me, my friend. We're not trying to pull the wool over anyone's eyes. We're positing no theories, offering no explanations, nor purporting to be anything we're not. The hoax argument belongs to the cynics who revel in debunking the many mad ideas that people come up with, all of which, I should add, are harmless. They're the ones causing damage by overlooking the beauty and poetry that is at play here, two things that neither the scientists and mathematicians nor the conspiracy theorists can explain away. Let their tongues wag; we're operating on a different plane, my brother.'

Redbone is touched by being called 'brother'; he notices such details, knows it is no accident. Being a man who is generally reserved or taciturn in social company, and who precedes any statement with a frown of contemplation, Calvert's words carry import and weight; much more so than his own. Redbone senses Calvert considering his next words even more carefully than usual.

'Most importantly of all, we're drawing attention to the land itself,' says Calvert. 'Because, really, this isn't about the patterns or the crops, it's about the land. The *land*. It's about getting people to learn to love it so that they don't take it for granted, and then feel compelled to protect it. A soldier doesn't solely fight for his or her country because of blind loyalty; they have to believe in it. They – and when I say they I mean *we* – have to first be sold on the story, even if it does turn out to be pure fiction. They have to love the cause, believe they are of a higher moral standing than the enemy; they have to believe they are just and true and pure in intention. Even the average Nazi foot soldier would have thought he was improving the world to begin with. You've seen it yourself: one day soon they'll try and build bypasses around Avebury and tunnels under Stonehenge. There'll be car parks and truck stops and cafes and gift shops. They've already fenced it off. Nearly five thousand years the 'Henge has stood there, and only now we can't be trusted to go near it. Just wait, they'll be driving cars up mountains and charging folk to jump into lakes. Profit, that's all they care about – not soil or stones or hills or holloways. If we let the bloodless cadavers in government have their way, Alton Kellett, White Whattle, Bracklebury, High Bassett and all the rest of them will be the names of shopping centres and drive-through fast-food places and power stations, all built where once there was nothing but natural landscapes and two daft lads making circles in the crop. They believe in money but we believe in something greater: truth and beauty. That will put us on the right side of history. Besides which, to lynch us they'd have to catch us first.'

Redbone cannot recall Calvert ever speaking quite so passionately about the subject – or indeed any subject – as he just has. Only now does he begin to truly understand how deep his friend's passion for the art form, the mission, runs. He has articulated it better than Redbone ever could.

'Have you ever thought about becoming a politician?' says Redbone.

'Go piss up a pylon,' says Calvert.

O

They walk out into the fields, swaddled by the crop that surrounds them. There is nothing else out here. No landmarks, no lights.

There are no distant houses or barns as markers to anchor them; there are not even wires or modern white windmills farming energy from the ether. Only crop and sky, dirt and stars.

'By the way,' says Calvert, 'this place we're heading to. It has no name.'

'No name?'

'Not that I'm aware of.'

'Everywhere has a name.'

'That's not true.'

'So where are we?'

'Broadly speaking, we are nowhere.'

'And specifically speaking?'

'Specifically speaking, we are definitely nowhere.'

'Nowhere?'

'Nowhere.'

Redbone is not happy with this response.

'But everywhere is somewhere,' he says with indignation.

'Well, technically, yes. Regions or areas can be named, but specific parts within them may not be. You can't name every inch of the land. This is one of them. It's just a field. Maybe the farmer has a name for it, just as he might have names for his cows or his pigs or each of the ducks in his duck pond that he dug six summers back – Mungo, Margo and Stella or whatever. Maybe he has names for his favourite trees too, the ones he has wandered past or sat under for all of his life. But there is no birth certificate for such things. Some names just exist on the tongues of those who frequent them. And this is just a nameless field not particularly close to anywhere significant.'

'It'll be significant tomorrow,' Redbone fires back. 'It'll be significant when tonight's pattern is front-page news. But if we can't name it in tribute to the location, then we'll have to call it The Circle With No Name.'

Now it is Calvert who is not happy with this prospect.

'That doesn't seem right. It seems almost disrespectful, in a way. Belittling.'

'Going by your logic, though, that's the way it is. How about Untitled (Crop Circle Number Nine)?'

'That's far too clinical. What do you call your design?'

'I thought I would name it Bronze Fox Mandala.'

'Well,' says Calvert, 'I think in this instance we can make an exception. Bronze Fox Mandala is perfect just as it is.'

They reach a wire fence and Calvert goes first, but as he straddles it a jolt of electricity shoots up his leading leg and through the arm and hand with which he grips the wire too, causing him to yelp in a high-pitched tone ill-suited to him, and then he falls tumbling over it, landing in a crumpled heap on the other side, his sunglasses skew-whiff on his face.

'Jesus f—'

Redbone slaps his thighs and roars with laughter. 'Did they teach you that technique in the SAS?'

Calvert looks bewildered as he picks himself up and wipes dust from his knees and elbows.

'Here, look,' says Redbone, stepping sideways for a few seconds until he reaches a wooden gate that they went straight past, and then walks up it as if it were a ladder, stands on the top bar, jams his hands in his pockets and, whistling a tune in a manner best described as vaudevillian, steps off into the part-darkness of the place with no name.

O

The Bronze Fox Mandala is inspired by the many geometric wonders of Hinduism and Buddhism, in which an ornate circular pattern is created in a square – in this case the field itself.

'Now I see why you chose this nowhere land,' says Redbone.

'It's the most perfectly perpendicular square field within a fifty-mile radius,' Calvert replies. 'There is a method to my madness, you know, just as there is to yours.'

As with many of the mandalas of ancient tradition, within the main circle are contained a series of diminishing squares, along with other details and flourishes designed to evoke a relaxing, somnambulistic feeling in all who gaze upon it – in this case, all being well, the readers of national newspapers. Some use mandalas as visual aids in which to lose themselves during meditation.

Redbone explained this to Calvert earlier in the summer in order to allow his friend enough time to source the correct location for what he had in mind.

'Why "Bronze Fox", though?' Calvert asked.

'He came to me in a dream,' replied Redbone. 'I envisioned a creature who was bronze in colour, and so regal and noble, and cunning too – a bit like us – that I knew I had to name something in his honour. And this is it.'

He hesitated then, savouring the moment.

'But in adopting two interwoven serpentine figures around the circle's perimeter, I've also added a Celtic twist. Here several cultures collide in perfect harmony. People who see this will hopefully feel both dazzled and becalmed because what we have here is an exercise in very gentle mass mind control. Do you like it?'

'Well,' replied Calvert, carefully assessing the pen-and-paper plan in front of him. 'In terms of scope and imagination, I didn't think it would be possible to better Cuckoo Spittle Thought Bubble, but then you surpassed yourself with the Throstle Henge Asteroid Necklace and my long-held suspicions about you were confirmed: you truly are a visionary beamed in from another dimension.'

Redbone grinned back.

'A berk, of course,' said Calvert. 'But a visionary berk.'

'I'll take that.'

O

'I've never known it this hot for this long.'

The men have paused for a brief break and sweat streaks their backs and brows. They both strip to their waists.

'Four in the morning and we're having to shed layers,' continues Redbone. 'Unbelievable.'

'The sun never sleeps and they say the planet is heating up,' says Calvert. 'They say we've burned a hole in the ozone layer with all our hairsprays and deodorants.'

'Not me,' says Redbone, indignant. 'I always used beer and sugar to spike my hair. And soap for my pits and bits.'

'Well, anyway. This is just the start of it. Scientists are predicting that in thirty or forty years' time this heat will become the new normal.'

Redbone whistles through his teeth. 'I mean, I love the summer but this doesn't feel right.'

'"Global warming", they call it, and it's entirely the fault of humans.'

'The crops are definitely suffering. And the animals. You can see it.'

'That's nothing. Crops can be watered and animals can be fed and cooled down and looked after. It's the wider ecological repercussions that will cause the real problems.'

'Such as?' asks Redbone.

'Such as the polar ice caps melting.'

'That won't happen. There's glaciers bigger than towns, ice shelves the size of countries. Icebergs like beautiful silent floating cathedrals.'

Redbone thinks of the icebergs that drift through his imagination in order to bring tranquillity to his more frantic and feverish moments.

'The thing is, it already *is* happening, my friend,' says Calvert. 'And where will all that ice go when it melts? Into the seas – seas that are already getting poisoned by pesticides and choked with waste. And where will the seas go when they rise? Onto the land.'

'Go on,' says Redbone.

'Well, Britain will shrink, for starters. The lowlands will be flooded fens. Species will suffer because the food chain will be broken. There'll be more extinctions, of course, new viruses will spread and snow will become a thing of the past too, something that will only exist on film and in the memories of those old enough to remember it. Imagine: no snow.'

'I love snow,' says Redbone in a low and mournful voice. 'I love everything about it. I used to keep snowballs in the freezer to throw at strangers in August, just to freak them out.'

Calvert draws his forearm across the sheen of beaded sweat on his tanned brow. He adjusts his sunglasses.

'We'll have to change our ways,' he continues. 'That much is certain. Mother Nature can take a lot of hammering but sooner or later she'll crack. Or strike back. It'll happen, trust me.'

'How will we know when that happens?'

'Oh, we'll know. Maybe she'll increase the frequency of the floods and send more landslides, spoil the crop worldwide for a few bad years. That's all it'll take. There's nothing like dusty broken limbs sticking out from rubble or the concave chests of starving children to instil a bit of perspective. Or perhaps a new strain of the mad cow disease will come along and strike us down, some virus that will embark upon a cruel and indiscriminate pruning, something to shave the population and cause us to have a rethink about how we live. It has happened plenty of times before, and it'll happen again. Everyone's heard of the Black Death. But the worst thing is, most people won't see it coming at all. They won't be ready. Especially in the cities, where they live like colonies of ants, all crawling on top of each other.'

Redbone scrunches his brow. 'That seems like a harsh prediction.'

'It stands to reason: the planet is heating up and unless changes are made there will be consequences. You can't leave an oven on forever.'

'What preparations are you talking about?'

'Oh, you know. The basics. Food, water, fuel. Weapons, if needed. Medicine, of course. Paracetamol will be like gold ingots when the going gets heavy, which it will, as things have expanded too quickly. And toilet paper, come to think of it.'

'I always thought it would be nuclear weapons that would be our downfall. My cousin was at Greenham Common.'

Calvert shakes his head. 'Don't need 'em,' he says adamantly. 'Don't need 'em. We had this conversation all the time in the Forces, and no military man wants to be around to witness the nuclear option. It's just senseless death on a mass scale. They'll never get used because they were only ever meant to be symbolic. A deterrent. People talk about how presidents have the codes to the nuclear weapons, but it's the military that runs that game, trust me. The presidents are kept in the dark where all that stuff is concerned; the rest is just bluff.'

He pauses and wipes his brow again.

'Me, I'm all set either way.'

'All set?'

'Of course,' says Calvert. 'I'm ready. The SAS might have taught me how to kill but it taught me how to live too. I've got my supplies ready. I've been stockpiling plenty of tinned food – meat and fruit, mainly – but also carbs, purification tablets and a few bits and pieces that you need for hunting, fire, that sort of thing. The survival basics.'

'But you live in the second-smallest house in England. Where do you store all this?'

Redbone sees Calvert visibly flinch at the fact that his house is not the smallest. He drops his voice to a conspiratorial level.

'I have them cached.'

'Where?'

'Where? Wouldn't you like to know.'

'Yes, I would.'

'Well, you can't. Get your own kidney beans.'

'Charming.'

'My stores are spread over a fifty-mile radius for safety, my friend. Their location is strictly on a need-to-know basis, marked only by memory. But don't worry, you'll be looked after when the time comes.'

'Well, that's nice, though I'm not a big fan of kidney beans. They make me bilious. On the bright side, at least there's still time to change things – to stop all this destruction that you're predicting.'

'I hope you're right. I hope there is still time.'

'Humans are stupid and greedy,' says Redbone, 'but, really, I doubt we'll let all that happen. I think things will be better in forty or fifty years' time.'

'I'm glad you're optimistic.'

'I have to be. Otherwise.'

'Otherwise what?'

Redbone shakes his head. For once his silence says enough.

O

As he works, Redbone loses himself again in the unexplored recesses of his active imagination. Calvert's proclamations have depressed him but as he walks he feels the ground beneath his feet and takes comfort in the solidity of it.

He knows there is something else under all this. He knows there exists an under-England, a chthonic place of hidden rivers and buried relics, of the bones of extinct animals and battle-slain bodies. Layer upon layer of it, laminations of land, each made from stories packed down tightly by the weight of time so that they become something else, just as wood becomes charcoal. So many stories, so many unseen footsteps. So many secrets that go beyond the limitations of the here and now.

He knows that their crop circles are fleeting and superficial, all surface, and quite useless, in a way, but he also knows that they matter because they are beautiful and nothing truly beautiful can be useless. It has taken him three summers, and now Calvert's assertion of their true relevance, to reach this revelation: that their beauty is their very purpose, and in just a matter of weeks they will no longer exist in the topsoil, in the barley and the wheat; they will no longer be visible from hill or helicopter, but instead will be one more story pressed down into the stratum.

A new layer of this under-England.

He also thinks about what would happen if all the world's dead and buried rose at once; what would happen were they suddenly tipped out of the graveyards like dusty dominoes from their box. Redbone thinks about how many people there would be if all the victims of that fatal disease known as time, from all countries, in all eras, clawed themselves out of the ground. What if the ashes of the immolated reassembled themselves into people too?

There would be far too many to fathom. There would be no place to put them either. The land mass would be entirely occupied and then they'd have to be thrown into the sea. Stacks of them, piled up. Underwater mountains of people, dead again.

These are the thoughts that Redbone chews over as he walks and works, weaving the Bronze Fox Mandala, his emotions fluctuating wildly in a way that is at odds with the true line that he treads.

O

As they depart, the two men know that tonight a new level of craftsmanship and artistry has been reached. The glass ceiling of achievement has been smashed with a sledgehammer of beauty – these are the exact words Redbone will later use. As far as they know, no mandala has ever been created on such a scale, and certainly not in a wheat field in a hot, dry corner of England over the course of one late-August night. It is surely a world record, though they care little for the officialdom that such an accolade suggests.

For now, they do not discuss it.

For now, they do not need to.

And also they cannot, for they both find themselves in a trance of sorts. Both men are in a sedated state of waking, walking meditation that is so satisfying that neither dares shatter it with something as limited and senseless as conversation. Exhausted, they instead drag their feet across the parched earth, their salty skin sodden with their own sweat, the taste of it strong on their lips and tongues, but as deeply satisfied as people can be when they know they have a purpose in the world.

The day breaks and the sun rises, and the Bronze Fox Mandala is unveiled, and even the sun itself is stunned by what it bears witness to. It beams blistering approval.

De nombreux cercles de culture sont apparus dans la campagne en Angleterre, ce qui a fait naître la croyance en une invasion de la Terre par des extraterrestres. Certains des motifs mesurent plusieurs centaines de mètres de diamètre, et selon des témoins sont des œuvres de beauté et d'émerveillement qui dépassent les capacités humaines.

Le Monde, 30 August 1989

Eine Reihe von Kornkreisen ist in England auf Feldern aufgetaucht, was zu der weit verbreiteten Überzeugung geführt hat, dass außerirdische Wesen die Erde übernehmen werden. Einige der Muster haben einen Durchmesser von mehr als hundert Metern und wurden von Zeugen als Werke von Schönheit und Wunder beschrieben, die weit über die menschlichen Fähigkeiten hinausgehen.

Die Zeit, 30 August 1989

在英格兰的田野里出现了许多麦田怪圈，导致人们普遍认为外星人将入侵地球。其中一些图案的长度和直径为数百英尺，目击者称其为精美的艺术品，其奇妙之处超出了人类的能力范围。

Reference News, 30 August 1989

Una serie de círculos de cultivos han aparecido en los campos de Inglaterra, lo que lleva a la creencia generalizada de que los extraterrestres invadirán la tierra. Algunos de los patrones miden más de cien metros de ancho y han sido descritos por testigos como obras de belleza y maravilla más allá de la capacidad humana.

El Correo, 30 August 1989

इंग्लैंड में खेतों में कई फसल चक्र दिखाई दिए है, जिससे व्यापक विश्वास पैदा हुआ कि धरती पर आक्रमण करने के लिए विदेशी है। कुछ पैटर्न लंबाई और व्यास में सैकड़ों फीट मापते है और गवाहों द्वारा सौंदर्य के कार्यों के रूप में वर्णित किया गया है और मानव क्षमता से काफी परे है। *Hindustan Dainik*, 30 August 1989

HONEYCOMB DOUBLE HELIX

For several days – in fact, weeks – it has felt as if his hand has been guided.

Nothing was premeditated, nothing planned.

Instead a stronger force slowly revealed the Honeycomb Double Helix, detail by detail, as he, Redbone, merely transcribed it. On different days he has worked on different sections, hunched over and lost in the moment. This is the big one.

He marvelled as it spread across the scroll of paper, admiring it as a visiting group of curious international art history students might a Francis Bacon in a major London gallery, and throughout it all he has been little more than a bystander to his own imagination's creation.

But was it even a product of his imagination? He thought not.

Because in those moments, alone in his van, Redbone understood that his ancestors were speaking through him. The voices of his past lives, and all past lives out in the fields and furrows, echoed onwards, and he was merely the receptacle, the passive but willing host. Thousands of years of mankind's collective experience of the land, of first roaming it, and then tilling and tending it, and lately poisoning and desecrating it – and forever gazing up at the cosmos too – were the true architects at work here.

Their hands clasped his and dragged lines of cheap blue biro ink across the paper, until Redbone gave himself over entirely to the Honeycomb Double Helix. He did not need tools such as rulers, protractors or compasses; everything was freehand.

Perhaps the universe itself, he wondered, with all its magical mathematics and alchemical collisions and collusions, was the driving force. Perhaps the magnetic fields of many moons were steering him, just as the earth's moon steers both the tides and the mysterious cycles of women.

Hours at a time passed this way, and time disintegrated. It fell away. The clock and the calendrical systems became archaic, irrelevant and myopic man-made functions as the concept for the crop circle that would crown the summer and stun an ailing world spread like a multitude of spiders' webs across the page. It was a design as intricate and expansive as Gaudí's blueprint for the Sagrada Família in Barcelona or Christopher Wren's plans for St Paul's Cathedral. It grew and grew, a web of wonder, then when day began to fade he would lay a blanket and board on the ground outside and work in the white circular glare of the headlights as bats swooped down from the nearby trees to feast upon the moths that mistook his headlights for twin moons.

Redbone did not notice them, for now he was inside the Honeycomb Double Helix. He was living it, breathing it.

Becoming it.

O

Harvest has made it harder for Calvert to source a location large enough to host something as grand as The Big One, as they have taken to calling it, as if they dare not even utter its name until it becomes a reality.

The drought has brought with it problems and already the farmers have cut a great deal of their crops. Each year for them is a high-wire balancing act dependent upon timing and deep knowledge of the terrain that is passed on down through the generations but is nevertheless ultimately dictated by the weather – specifically rain, or lack thereof. To harvest too early can mean a diminished yield, too late and the crop can spoil and be worthless.

So all across the country farmers watch the sky as if they were observing the final frame of a snooker game played upon a coarse blue baize, each trying to second-guess the next move of their blank-eyed opponent, the clouds. It is the great agricultural gamble, where tactics are at the mercy of other elements beyond their control.

Calvert spends his time exploring, each day a different direction, each field a potential blank canvas awaiting their magical touch.

He wanders and he watches, from fence posts to hilltops; occasionally he ponders what it would be like to see the land again from a helicopter as he once did often, but he also understands that to source a location in such a way would be entirely against the spirit of their creative endeavour. To do so would be no more authentic than a flock of fieldfares or redwings chartering a plane to North Africa during the English winter. In short: unthinkable and entirely against the natural order.

No. Their work must be done with their feet, eyes, hands and muscle memory alone.

One night during a reconnaissance Calvert comes across what may be the perfect pasture, but when he returns in the morning to view it in daylight it is busy with combine harvesters that have been out since first light, when the barley stalks are still moist, and the crop now lies in rows ready for bundling, drying, threshing and winnowing.

For it is September now and though the sun is a crock of burning gold and the sky a lake of fire, summer is already in its death throes, the languorous days shortening and the drought-hit land as dry as an abandoned library full of books dedicated entirely to dust.

Finally he finds a place that fulfils his criteria and where the creative conditions appear perfect. The crop is still a week or more away from harvest, the field is huge and gently slopes in such a way that any design will be able to be viewed in its full aspect from both a neighbouring field and a road that runs half a mile beyond it. The road leads to their village, in fact, only a few miles away in one direction, and to another village the opposite way, and then a town, and then a motorway, and then the rest of the county, the country, continent, world and cosmos.

And it is to the cosmos that they are speaking now, because on this sun-soaked Saturday evening in early September, an anonymous field is, for two strange men at least, the centre of the universe.

O

For once Redbone arrives early, sleep-famished but practically clattering with excess energy. His mind is a thousand ball bearings in a biscuit tin.

Calvert is standing stooped beneath the stone lintel of the low doorway of Bluebell Cottage, looking out across the square. He too is packed and ready.

Both men feel within themselves a differing rhythm driving their hearts and pumping their blood until it feels itchy in their veins, but once they are out in the field those rhythms will adjust themselves accordingly and fall into step, so that they lock together as one pulse that beats with the rhythms of the turning earth, the setting sun and the wax and wane of the moon.

It is a not insignificant moment when Calvert invites Redbone into his tiny house, and equally significant is Redbone's acceptance, though of course neither remarks upon the fact because they are men of a certain breed, and men of a certain breed do not dig deep into the trench of sentimentality. All emotional drawbridges remain up. It is easier that way. Some things do not need identifying through expression in order to exist.

Indeed, only three words are exchanged before Redbone unrolls his scroll to reveal his masterwork.

'Come in.'

'Thanks.'

O

They eat beforehand in the VW so that every spare second of the summer night can be used for maximum potential.

Calvert opens a plastic tub and offers it to Redbone. He takes it and peers inside.

'What are these?'

'Cornish-style pasties.'

'What's in them?'

Calvert hesitates.

'Foraged ingredients.'

'That's disconcertingly imprecise. Is this what you ate in the war?'

'What you have here is a culinary delight that is about as local as food can get. And, no, we didn't.'

'Such as?'

'Such as mushrooms. Sorrel. Spinach. Hazelnuts. Buckthorn berries. Primrose.'

'All together?'

'I'm not finished. There's also bilberries. Sweet chestnut. New potatoes. Dandelion. Mallow flowers. Yarrow.'

'OK. So . . .' Redbone hesitates. 'Is it sweet or savoury?'

'A bit of both. It's a two-course meal in one pasty. I made the pastry myself.'

Redbone tears off a corner, hesitates, and then puts it in his mouth. He tentatively chews it slowly, like a blindfolded cow. He swallows and takes a moment to reach a verdict. He smacks his lips.

'What makes it Cornish?'

'I don't know,' says Calvert. 'The idea of it?'

'I've tasted nothing like it.'

He takes another bite.

'Thanks, I think. How are you feeling?'

'Feeling?' says Redbone, surprised at the question.

'Yes.'

'How am I *feeling*?'

'Yes.'

'You never talk about feelings. Are you alright?'

'Never better.'

'So why do you ask?'

'Well,' says Calvert, 'you've spent weeks working on the ultimate crop circle design, our last of the summer. Your masterwork. And so now, as a friend, I'm asking how you are feeling about it all.'

Redbone is touched. He swallows again, and it is like swallowing soil, then he thinks the question over.

'I feel – '

'Yes?'

'I feel – '

'Go on.'

'I feel bigger than God. I feel *ready*.'

He offers the tub of pasties back to Calvert.

Calvert recoils, his face displaying disgust, yet the scar tissue is unmoving, a frozen reminder.

'No chance.'

O

It had happened in a brief flash of blue followed by silence.

Then ringing. Piercing ringing. His head had been an anvil struck by a cold sledgehammer in a hot forge, and one side of his face, one cheek, was peeled away in a neat flap of flesh like the skin of a perfectly ripe orange. It was dangling there, damp on his chin, and at first he went to bat it away before he realised it was part of him. Calvert remembers thinking that it seemed so obvious – corny, almost – to be nearly blown apart like that, so unexpectedly but also so predictably, as if he were watching a film of himself. It was embarrassing too, in a way, because here he was, a member of an elite and secretive trained force, felled by an improvised device dug shallow into the soil by a two-bit enemy military operation.

There was mud and smoke and the damp pack on his back was suddenly so heavy, and Calvert crumpled to his knees as the slowly growing siren of himself wailed silently inside. And in that moment the stupid war, and all the philosophies that justify war, became utterly meaningless. He was lucky to have his legs, they said. Lucky to have his face and his sight and most of his teeth and his fractured jaw still in one piece. Lucky to be alive, they said. But a piece of him, a big shapeless shadow-piece of him, was still there now, quivering with fear in the damp and viscid dirt.

O

Sunset occurs at 19:46 and it rises again at 06:26, so ten hours and forty minutes is the length of time that it takes for two skilled and experienced men in good physical condition – one with a pragmatic and disciplined disposition born from years of military training, the other prone to visions which he is somehow able to capture in print – to create the world's first Honeycomb Double Helix.

They pause only to drink water, otherwise every moment of the long, still night is spent marking, measuring, walking and flattening the dozens of small circles that join together to make two intertwined spiralling lines, each of which features multiple peaks and troughs, and which together create a twisting corkscrew effect. More than anything, it resembles the coiled chains of the double helix that forms the genetic structure of human DNA.

Only when the pattern is nearly completed does Redbone reveal this to Calvert.

'You must have done a hell of a lot of research to create this,' says the latter, tipping his metal army flask to his parched mouth.

'Nope,' replies Redbone.

'But you must at least have looked at a hell of a lot of scientific material.'

Redbone shakes his head vociferously. 'No. None.'

'Then how – '

'I don't know.'

Redbone takes the flask from his friend, drinks and then continues.

'I don't know. It just arrived on the page. Maybe this thing has been within me all along. Perhaps I have been carrying the Double Helix inside me for all of my life, or even earlier. Maybe it comes from somewhere far more deeply rooted, from ten thousand life-times ago, from all lives lived, in all places. Perhaps this pattern is the very essence of humankind, and I am just the receptable, the conduit, and together we – you and me – are little more than the midwives tasked with delivering it all the way from a subatomic level and out onto, and *into*, the land.'

Calvert has nothing to say, for this revelation, and their combined achievement, is once again beyond words. And, though he dare not admit it, he thinks that were he to speak in this moment he might start crying. And if he started crying he might never stop. And that would just be far too much for either of them to have to face.

But The Big One is just so beautiful.

Instead he clears his throat, adjusts his sunglasses and grunts, 'We should crack on.'

As an added flourish – and purely because they can – the two men fill the spaces created between the main stems with a honeycomb pattern made from dozens of hexagons, each measuring the same precise dimensions. The combination of circles and hexagons presented Redbone with all sorts of geometric quandaries and conundrums during planning that had to be solved in order to retain the integrity, continuity and energy flow throughout. To do so also required working on a scale far beyond any of their previous creations – bigger than Trapping St Edmunds Solstice Pendulum, bigger than Cuckoo Spittle Thought Bubble, bigger even than Untitled (Bronze Fox Mandala).

The added hexagonal embellishment alone, a design which only a year or two ago would have constituted a full night's work, is now little more than an indulgent exercise in showboating, a victory lap for tomorrow's awestruck worldwide audience.

As they finish the final set of internal patterning, Redbone's calculations tell them that the Honeycomb Double Helix measures nine hundred feet from end to end. It is nearly three times as long as Big Ben is high, twice the height of the Great Pyramid of Giza in Egypt, and much the same length as the Eiffel Tower were it to be laid down right here in the wheat crop of a fading English summer.

It is still night – just – when they separately flatten the final hexagons in the central part of the Helix, to complete the last section of honeycomb.

'This will never be bettered,' says Redbone to himself, and as the sun peeks over the brow, their legs feel like rotten trees fit for felling and their arms are widow-makers waiting to fall. They ache all over and the empty caves of their minds hold nothing but the bleached bones of their grunting ancestors and the occasional roosting bat.

This is happiness.

This is living.

O

Smoke singes the night air. It is out of place. Smoke is the scent of decay and the burning-away of the last shortening days of the season's closing circle. Smoke is the scent of autumn, of purge and clearance. Smoke is the scent of all lived things passing. Of death.

But it is not autumn and the land is not yet ready for death. It is not ready for purging and clearance. The soil is still fertile and good. It has harboured millions of seeds – more seeds than there are people on the planet – and it alone has nurtured them through sun and rain, and now the crop is strong and set for the last push of harvest. Soon it will be a time of celebration. In these coming days the last of the wheat will be cut down and gathered up, then processed to a powder to be stirred into a mix to be placed into one hundred thousand burning ovens.

A song begun in summer will warm the winter through.

The Honeycomb Double Helix is complete. Tonight, laid bare in the flattened crop, is the manifestation of two minds that first dared to imagine, and then acted upon this need to express. Their discipline has remained steadfast, and their motivations pure throughout.

Redbone and Calvert separate to coil the lengths of rope, remove the pegs and collect the planks that they have scattered across the field. Exhausted and silent, they know they are nothing but that the Honeycomb Double Helix is everything. Beside it they feel insignificant, small and worthless, as they hope all people will.

Tomorrow they can assume that it will be photographed from land and air. It will be discussed on radio and recorded on film; it will be documented in occultist pamphlets and academic journals. Satellites will receive it and it will cross seas. The Honeycomb Double Helix will be broadcast around the spinning planet, and will be seen in France and Japan and Mexico and Sweden and Russia and Argentina and a hundred other countries besides.

And its unveiling without ceremony will mark the end of one life and the beginning of another, because after this a whole new phase of crop circles is certain to follow. Something once pure will soon become tainted by ego, competition and conjecture. The purity and mystery of the endeavour will be irreversibly tainted, polluted, corrupted.

Their nostrils detect the bitter sting of burning before their waking minds acknowledge its closeness: smoke on a zephyr unseen, drifting idly across the nodding heads of wheat, each hanging heavy with life and potential.

Calvert straightens first and sniffs the air like a creature. He turns one way and then the other, seeking a visual source. Hundreds of hobbled miles trail behind him in lines and circles, in whirlpools and whales, pathways and pendulums, snowflakes and spinners, necklaces, caterpillars and keys. And now, in the Honeycomb Double Helix too.

He sees the chimney of smoke rising like a pillar of stone, solid in appearance, sculptural. It is the same colour as the last few minutes of the many summer nights that he has come to understand every tone and texture of.

But then it bends to the breeze and steers towards him.

He drops the rope. He drops the plank.

His feet are rooted to the ground and for one long torturous moment he does not move.

Far away Redbone smells it too. The acrid tang of something burning.

At much the same time, from opposite ends of the field, they hear the rising roar and hot crackle of infernal destruction. Calvert runs and Redbone runs. They each run towards the flames that rise licking at the sky and blazing through the crop of wheat.

And from the crop come fleeing towards them in the opposite direction an entire animal population shrieking and squeaking in fear. Hares, hedgehogs, rabbits, mice, deer. Foxes and badgers that were passing through. Stoats and weasels. Birds too, hundreds of birds taking flight when they ought to be roosting, rising up collectively on the warm updraughts created by the raging conflagration below.

The flames circle round and change direction, and Redbone sees that many of the animals will at least be safe. The slowing of the fire gives them an advantage in the stampede as they seek the shortest route.

In the flames, in the roaring heat, Redbone sees something.

His future.

It is one step removed from being recognisable. It is scorched black.

He is someone else there, and the sun is slowly dying.

No birds sing.

Calvert nearly collides with him and in the light of the encroaching fire they each see that the other's illuminated face is already soot-marked and sweat-streaked. The masks of themselves have fallen away, just as man's mask falls away when he finds himself exposed in conflict as mortar shells crack and bullets riddle the turf around him, or when he is lost in a deep-time vision. They are too stunned for questions.

A wall of flame advances towards them, eating up the Honeycomb Double Helix, and all they can do is be like the animals that they are, and run.

Some say that crop circles are the markings left behind following alien visitation, while others dismiss them as the work of pranksters—or what one British public figure has dubbed "dusk devils."

But whatever your belief, dozens of these mysterious patterns have appeared overnight in crops of wheat and barley over the course of this summer in the south-west counties of England, and experts worldwide have been left scratching their heads at this growing phenomenon.

Though crop circles have been sighted in previous years, it was in late spring of this year that they began to appear with increased regularity in the agricultural lands that lie west of London, England. The designs are so complex, vast, and mathematically proficient that theories abound as to not only the reasons for their creation, but also who or what is behind them.

The summer of mysterious activity reached a peak this weekend when hundreds of acres of prime wheat fields were set ablaze, causing hundreds of thousands of pounds' worth of damage in lost produce in the lead-up to the annual harvest, with many leading investigators of the paranormal now offering the fires as concrete proof that crop circles are the work of unknown beings from other planets.

"The fire was started by an alien transport system that had temporarily landed in wheat fields," says Kyle D. Lubbock of the Wisconsin Institute of Paranormal Research. "Upon leaving the scene, excess heat generated by this 'spaceship'—for want of a better term—scorched the crop, which was in its driest state following a drought in the area, and consequently ignited a fire. Whether this was an act of aggression or an accident remains open to interpretation. Having personally examined the site, however, an outline of this spaceship, which is a complex structure incorporating both corkscrew and hexagonal patterns, can clearly be seen in the darker scorch marks imprinted in the earth, and which therefore were clearly created at a heat greater than that of the fire that followed. Abstract fragments of molten metal and fibers from a ropelike substance were also left on the site, perhaps as a form of communication, and which suggest that the visitors come from a planet with natural resources similar to ours."

The New Yorker, 15 September 1989

They drive in silence, the heat at their backs.

Even when the scorched remains of the field that housed the Honeycomb Double Helix are far behind them, and the sound of sirens has been reduced to a hollow haunted ringing in their ears, they can still feel the torrid sweltering heat of the wall of fire as it advanced towards them.

Worst of all was the disturbance to all those creatures that had made their habitation in the brilliant flaxen acreage of crops. The biblical images of the animals fleeing in fear for their lives, and the sounds they made, will stay with them both for a long time. True trauma.

'It wasn't us, was it?' says Redbone finally. 'Please tell me it wasn't us, Ivan.'

Calvert chews the inside of his mouth and shakes his head.

'It can't have been. We carry nothing that's combustible or capable of starting fire. We never would.'

'Because it's in the code?'

'Because it's in the code.'

'And,' adds Calvert, 'we were nowhere near it when it started. A fire like that, in those crops, at this time of year, would take in seconds. Whatever – or whoever – started it must have been close by. They had to be.'

They fall into silence once more, both with their eyes trained to the winding back lanes that they make sure they stick to. But really they are not watching the road; instead they are both lost in thought as they try to bring sense and order to rapidly scrambling minds.

'We were so close,' says Redbone, gripping the steering wheel. '*So close*. The Honeycomb Double Helix was practically done. We nearly had it. We were minutes away from completion of the greatest crop circle ever created.'

'It doesn't matter,' says Calvert, suddenly feeling more tired than he has ever felt in his life. Gravity is pulling him downwards.

He removes his sunglasses, swills water from his flask and with one hand washes his face with it.

It is the second time recently that Redbone has seen his friend's eyes, which are rimmed red from the hot sting of the smoke. Calvert rubs soot from the silver scar. He scrubs at it with his cuff. He takes a long swig and swallows, and his Adam's apple is a small hard lump flexing in his throat. He passes the flask to his friend and instructs him to do the same.

'None of that matters any more,' says Calvert.

'I suppose there's always next week. We can always try it again next week somewhere else far from here.'

Calvert does not reply.

'Can't we?'

Calvert slowly shakes his head.

'Harvest is next week. The farmers and their crews will be out and the fields will be clipped and stripped and then summer will be over. Then it will be autumn. Then it will be winter.'

They drive on.

'Next year, then?' says Redbone, turning to him, his bloodshot eyes searching, hoping, pleading.

Again his friend does not reply.

ACKNOWLEDGEMENTS

Thank you to: early readers Kathryn Myers, Cally Callomon and Charlie Cooper. Carol Gorner and the Gordon Burn Trust, in whose house this book was written. Terry Lee, Allegra Le Fanu, Paul Baggaley and all at Bloomsbury. Thanks to Greg Heinimann for the artwork and Silvia Crompton for the eagle-eyed copyedit. David Atkinson. Saul Adamczewski and Dan McEvoy. Annette Weber, Torsten Woywod and everyone at DuMont. My agent Jessica Woollard for the invaluable support and encouragement, and Clare Israel, Alice Howe, Margaux Vialleron, Penelope Killick and all at David Higham Associates.

And especially Adelle Stripe.

ACKNOWLEDGMENTS

A NOTE ON THE AUTHOR

Benjamin Myers was born in Durham in 1976. His most recent novel, *The Offing*, was an international bestseller and selected for the Radio 2 Book Club. Other works include *The Gallows Pole* which won the Walter Scott Prize for historical fiction and is being adapted for a six-part TV series co-produced by the BBC and A24, directed by Shane Meadows; *Beastings* which was awarded the Portico Prize for Literature; and *Pig Iron* which won the inaugural Gordon Burn Prize. He has also published non-fiction, poetry and crime novels and his journalism has appeared in publications including the *Guardian*, *New Statesman*, *Spectator*, *Caught by the River* and many more. He lives in the Upper Calder Valley, West Yorkshire.

benmyers.com / @BenMyers1

A NOTE ON THE TYPE

The text of this book is set Adobe Garamond. It is one of several versions of Garamond based on the designs of Claude Garamond. It is thought that Garamond based his font on Bembo, cut in 1495 by Francesco Griffo in collaboration with the Italian printer Aldus Manutius. Garamond types were first used in books printed in Paris around 1532. Many of the present-day versions of this type are based on the *Typi Academiae* of Jean Jannon cut in Sedan in 1615.

Claude Garamond was born in Paris in 1480. He learned how to cut type from his father and by the age of fifteen he was able to fashion steel punches the size of a pica with great precision. At the age of sixty he was commissioned by King Francis I to design a Greek alphabet, and for this he was given the honourable title of royal type founder. He died in 1561.